I0589122

TELEVANGELIST

RON JOHNSON

Golden Calf Books

Copyright © 2017 Ron Johnson

The moral right of the author has been asserted.

All rights reserved.
No part of this publication may be reproduced, stored in a retrieval system, or transmitted, in any form or by any means, without the prior permission in writing of the publisher, nor be otherwise circulated in any form of binding or cover other than that in which it is published and without a similar condition including this condition being imposed on the subsequent purchaser.

Published by Golden Calf Books

Print ISBN 978-0-692-87663-3

Cover Art Concept: Som-usa Charuchinta
Cover Art Designer: Pintado www.pintado.weebly.com

Discuss the book with other readers and stay updated on future releases at the Televangelist Facebook page: facebook.com/televangelistbook/

Typesetting services by BOOKOW.COM

To the world
An offering

Epigraph

'Cause our income last year was over a hundred million dollars.
-Televangelist Kenneth Copeland speaking at the KCM Ministers'
Conference

CONTENTS

GENESIS

A once-blistering desert sun hangs low in the sky behind the prison compound. Outside the release gate, a pudgy, balding man stands next to a well-driven Buick Park Avenue and checks his watch—it's 4:20 p.m., twenty minutes past the scheduled release time. The delay is most assuredly due to prison staff since the man's brother has always been punctual.

The gate clinks as a guard opens it. A hand extends from inside the gate and shakes the guard's hand as distant words are exchanged. A handsome fortyish man in a tailored red suit exits the gate cupping a Bible and inhaling a couple lungfuls of free air. He sees the pudgy man and smiles warmly. Bart Baxter begins walking toward the car as the pudgy man, his brother Luke Baxter, smiles back.

Luke calls out, "Looks like you got the suit I sent you?"

Bart looks down at his suit and adjusts the cuffs. "The safe travels of this here suit cost me ten packs of Ramen, a bag of moonshine, and my anal virginity."

Luke raises his eyebrows quizzically at Bart.

"And that was just to bribe the guards!" jokes Bart.

Both men laugh and hug.

Luke confides, "It's good to see you brother."

"Good to see you too man."

The two men separate as Bart asks, "So how's business?"

"Business is bad Bart. We're barely pulling any offerings and the last five tithes have been chewing gum."

"How many people are left in the pews?"

Luke doesn't have to think. "Fifty-three."

Bart scratches his chin as he replies, "That's good Luke. *Real good.*"

Luke squints at Bart, "Why is that good?"

Bart taps his Bible then turns back toward the prison gates. "Because I've just spent four years reading the Good Book, dear brother."

Bart raises his hands to the sky as he looks at the prison.

"And as God is my witness," Bart pauses before raising his voice in triumph, "I have been born again!"

Bart stares out over the prison then turns back to his pudgy brother Luke.

"Now let's make some money."

The men load up in Luke's car and belt in. Luke floors the gas pedal and the '98 Buick lurches forward past a sign reading *Interstate 15 – 8 miles.*

* * *

With the moon low in the sky and rising quickly, the Buick carrying the Brothers' Baxter turns off the highway and quickly finds its way through a neighborhood full of minivans and picket fences to a home like all the rest.

Luke pulls into the driveway and leaves the engine running as he turns to Bart, "So I'll see you on Sunday morning?"

Bart flashes a rare look of uncertainty at Luke. "That kinda depends on how this goes tonight with Julie."

Luke reassures his little brother, "It'll be fine Bart."

Bart isn't so sure. "I hope so."

"Hey, she said you could stay with her. That's a start right?"

"Yeah but the start of *what?*" Bart says.

Both men laugh nervously before Bart shoulders the door open and exits the car.

As Luke pulls out of the driveway he yells to Bart, "Sunday morning nine o'clock. Don't forget!"

Bart nods his understanding.

Luke drives off as Bart walks to a front door illuminated by a porch light shining white. He tries the knob to find it unlocked, a positive omen. Bart walks into the house.

Inside the master bedroom, Julie is putting new sheets on a king-sized bed. Bart arrives in the doorway and knocks softly on the door.

"Can I help?"

Julie doesn't skip a beat as she continues stretching and yanking at the sheets. "Oh you've helped enough already," she says.

Bart sighs in discouragement.

Julie turns around to face his direction and offer a warm smile.

"Welcome home Bart."

Julie approaches Bart and hugs him. Relieved, Bart awkwardly returns the hug. Julie kisses him on the cheek and pulls away as Bart remarks as gently as he can about the elephant in the room.

"I figured you'd still be mad at me."

"I *was* still mad at you up until you walked in the door. Now it's time to turn the page and start fresh." Julie has always lived in the moment.

"But Bart, I have to tell you something." Her eyes make a plea. "I didn't wait this long just so the past could repeat itself."

"Don't wor—"

Julie interrupts Bart as her heartache reveals itself in words. "No Bart, listen to me. I've waited four years for you. I've worked, I've paid the bills, and I've crawled into this bed every night alone. You can't do this to me again. Do you understand what I'm saying?"

Ashamed, Bart replies, "I understand. Bart's staying on this side of the law from now on."

Julie's face suddenly flashes anger. "No Bart, that's not what I'm talking about! I don't care about the law and I don't care about prison. I care about you cheating on me."

Julie adds, "Break any law you want except mine. Don't break *my* law, Bart."

Bart's face turns red but Julie has already been embarrassed enough. If Bart's embarrassed now, that's *too damn bad*.

Julie looks directly into Bart's shame-filled eyes and gives him a stern warning. "You can't cheat on me again Bart. Never again."

"I understand. That will never happen again."

Julie pounces on him, "Never?"

Bart returns Julie's stare. *"Never."*

Julie finally accepts Bart's show of submission and lowers the intensity. "Shake on it?"

Bart and Julie shake hands on the deal.

Julie returns to her playful self, at Bart's expense. "And since you just came home from cootie-land, you're sleeping on the couch tonight big fella."

Bart happily nods his acceptance and leaves the room.

Julie shouts through the door at him, "There's some food in the fridge if you're hungry."

Bart shouts back, "Okay!"

The sound of cabinets opening and closing rings down the hallway as Bart rifles through them like a bear searching for honey. A shout is heard from the kitchen.

"Hey do you got any Ramen?"

A Very Special Man

It's 8:45 a.m. on a cloudy Sunday morning outside Pastor Luke Baxter's dilapidated church, Salvation Alley. Through the cracked glass of the church sign reads the same uninspiring message that's existed there for months:

> *Salvation Alley and Pastor Luke Baxter welcome you every Sunday morning at 10am.*

In the church's gravelly parking lot, Pastor Baxter's '98 Buick is parked a few spaces down from an ancient Datsun with a dust layer so thick it's preserved the paint. Mini blinds are drawn over a second-story window looking out over the empty lot. On the other side of the window sits Pastor Luke Baxter, clad in an old sportcoat and brown slacks that fit him poorly when he first bought them. Now, years later, the fit has only gotten worse.

Pastor Baxter is busy reviewing his sermon notes when a door knock interrupts him. Luke calls to the door, "Yeah?"

The head usher peeks his oily head through the door. Luke knows him as Phil, but beyond that he doesn't care. He knows the ushers only work the gig to earn better seating assignments in Heaven and he doesn't particularly like any of them.

"Mrs Christianson called and said she's not feeling well this morning."

Luke looks annoyed. "Okay."

Usher Phil leaves the doorway as Luke mutters to himself, "Crap."

The door suddenly opens wide and Bart Baxter enters the office. He's wearing the same red suit he wore when he left prison two days ago, freshly cleaned and pressed, and his hair is immaculate. He looks like a VIP-ticket holder to *his own show.*

Bart notices Luke's annoyed look and inquires, "What's up?"

"My biggest donor isn't coming in today.

"Oh? Who's that?"

"Mrs Christianson."

Bart remembers Grace Christianson from decades ago. She was old then too. "Ah yes, the widow Christianson. She's still chugging along huh?"

Luke appends Bart's comment, "Chugging along and keeping this church afloat for the last fifty years."

Bart quickly updates his mental file on Mrs Christianson. "Well don't you worry dear brother, the Heavenly Spirit is in the air of this old church."

Bart holds his Bible aloft while smiling. "God is smiling on us, Luke. He even gave me a vision in the joint."

Luke laughs dismissively at Bart. "A vision huh? Of what, exactly?"

Bart's eyes flash with excitement, *"Money."*

The boys laugh as Luke responds, "Okay Billy Graham just hold your horses there. You're ready for today right?"

A look of disbelief paints Bart's face as he raises his arms to shoulder level and looks down at his own suit.

"Luke," Bart pauses as confidence oozes from every pore, *"do I look ready?"*

Luke's anxiety rises with Bart's confidence. He's not sure if his small church is ready for the Supreme Being known as Bart Baxter.

"Oh boy," Luke says with a nervous sigh.

Bart revels in making his big brother uncomfortable. He spins around slowly to show off his suit of confidence as Luke stares at him. Bart begins dancing a jig as Luke sighs again.

"Oh boy…"

* * *

A light rain takes parishioners by surprise as they arrive inside the church and sniff out their regular pews. With only fifteen minutes until the service begins, attendance is nowhere near capacity in the two hundred seat church.

Clutching a Bible, Bart has been manning the nave door and chatting with arriving parishioners. Some elderly churchgoers remember him from earlier years. Fresher faces who've never seen him before are excited as the handsome, dapper man greets each and every one of them before they pass down the aisles.

At present, Bart is schmoozing the eighty-something Mrs Grace Evans. "Well it is a delight to see you again Mrs Evans, you look just the same as I remembered you. It's as if time stands still in this wonderful little church of ours!"

Mrs Evans chuckles to herself. "Tell that to Mr Evans."

"Oh yes I remember Mr Evans, is he not feeling well today?"

Mrs Evans' voice rises slightly, "He's dead!"

Bart blinks once on the outside and once on the inside, but quickly recovers. "Oh I'm so sorry to hear that. He was a lovely man."

Mrs Evans waves Bart off and begins a tiny but impassioned rant. "Oh, lovely to you maybe! To me he was just one big, dopey, fartin' machine. The house smelled like a fart factory after forty years of him tootin' off all the time!"

Bart lets a small, unobtrusive laugh escape as he looks around uncomfortably for a way to exit the conversation.

"Oh well I'm sure your house smells nice and fresh Mrs Evans."

Mrs Evans steps on Bart's reassuring words, "Nice and fresh, yeah sure *now it is* after Fred isn't around to go farti—"

Bart opts for the universal conversation ender: the watch check. He eyes his wrist and interrupts.

"Oh Mrs Evans, I'm sorry I need to get back to meet with my brother before the service begins. I forgot to mention, we need to pray for Mrs Christianson this week." Bart feigns sadness. "She's not feeling well."

A derailed Mrs Evans nods. She wasn't done ranting about Mr Evans and his gas issues, in fact she could go on for hours about it, but she understands that Bart has church business to attend to. She pats his arm in agreement and sends him retreating back toward the stage.

As Mrs Evans takes her seat, she pulls out a notepad and writes on it: *Pray for Mrs Christianson.*

* * *

Standing in front of his office mirror, Pastor Luke Baxter uses a wide-toothed comb to put the final touches on what remains of his hair. Bart enters the office and looks at Luke's mirrored reflection.

"It's not gonna get any better Luke, just let it be."

Luke is mildly annoyed at Bart. Men with hair have no business giving styling instructions to men without. "Yeah well just let me do what I have to do with it. I have a method."

Bart laughs heartily and Luke chuckles in response as he gingerly combs the little dangler at the front of his scalp all the way to the back, where it will no longer dangle—it will *rest.*

"If I don't get it just right it'll flop down in front of my face."

Bart stares at Luke in the mirror as he fusses with his hair. Luke finally finishes combing and looks side-to-side to verify his handiwork. *"Bullseye."*

Bart humors him, "Hey it looks good man!"

"Thank you," Luke replies smugly, still eyeing the mirror.

With all Baxter hairs in place, Bart changes the subject to the sermon. "Now when you introduce me, don't say anything about prison. Just say I was away for awhile."

Luke nods, "Okay."

"And don't forget to put out the prayer request for Mrs Christianson. We need to keep our *money train* chugging along."

Luke looks disapprovingly at Bart. Money train or not, Mrs Grace Christianson is still a loyal member of the church and should be afforded some dignity.

Recognizing that he went a tad too far, Bart backpedals. "Okay, maybe that was a bit harsh."

Luke stares at Bart with eyebrows raised. "Is that all, coach?" Luke asks sarcastically.

"Yes that's all. Go get 'em."

Slipping into his old sportcoat, Luke tells Bart, "I've been doing this crap for over ten years now, Bart. I think I know how to do it by now."

Bart looks judgmentally around the stuffy, dated office. "Yeah I can see that," he says underwhelmingly.

Luke ignores the comment and heads out the door.

"Oh wait Luke!"

Annoyed, Luke returns to the door. *"What,* Bart?"

Bart looks at Luke and pumps an imaginary train whistle with his arm, *"Bwoop-Bwoop!"*

* * *

The Organist plays soft fill music as Pastor Luke Baxter finishes up the opening prayer. Except for Pastor Luke, all heads are bowed and all eyes closed, including those of the Organist. Luke peeks through squinted eyes at his notes resting on the pulpit.

"...and finally Lord, we keep Grace Christianson in our thoughts as she's been bothered with a terrible chill this weekend. We ask that you keep her warm and dry this week in a *cocoon* of divine protection ..."

A deep voice from within the congregation calls out warmly, "Yes, Lord."

"...so that she may continue in her *planetary service* to you."

Offstage, Bart cocks his head and looks sideways, perplexed by his brother's strange prayer.

"In Jesus' name we pray,"

Pastor Baxter and his congregation speak together in agreement, "Amen!"

Luke claps once to end the prayer and move forward with the sermon. He addresses his congregation in the familiar pastorly cadence.

"Brothers and sisters, I'd like to introduce a very special man to you. This person is a good man. He is a humble man. He is kind... he is warm...and he is God-fearing."

The congregation tunes-in tightly to Pastor Luke.

"And this man has a wonderful message of repentance and salvation to deliver. Salvation Alley, please welcome home my kid brother, Pastor Bart Baxter!"

The small congregation applauds lightly as Bart, just offstage, makes eye contact with the Organist. Bart nods to her and begins his walkout as she softly plays a triumphant tune.

Bart walks to Luke and the two embrace at the pulpit. Smiling widely, Bart pulls back and looks squarely at a teary-eyed Luke. Bart's own eyes moisten in response. They embrace once more as the congregation rise to their feet and applaud further.

As the men let go of one another and separate, Luke pats Bart encouragingly on the arm.

"Good luck," Luke says off-mic.

Luke walks offstage as Bart steps up to the pulpit, dabbing at his eyes.

"Wow, I didn't expect that," Bart says, slightly overcome at the sight of his brother's tears.

The congregation offers up a friendly laugh.

"Well, I'd like to introduce myself to all you fine folks. I'm Bart Baxter and my father was Pastor James Baxter. Some of you might have known him..."

Bart continues speaking as the congregation listens attentively.

* * *

The church clock reads 10:40 a.m. Bart has been speaking for twenty minutes and is nearing the end of his sermon. He's speaking with fire now; the congregation is mesmerized by him.

"...but every second I spent in that prison cell was a second I spent closer to God. Because *God* is who sentenced me to live in that cell all those years, not *some man* callin' himself a judge!"

A voice from the congregation shouts, "Amen!"

"For there's only *one judge* in this world, and that's *the Lord God Jesus Christ!*"

A different voice shouts, "Praise Jesus!"

Bart hits them with his finale, "And I'd do it *all again tomorrow* if the Lord God judged it so!"

A chorus of *Amens* hail from the congregation as Bart pauses for his final line to sink in. He smiles across the congregation. They love him.

Pastor Luke enters the stage clapping. He slowly approaches Bart at the pulpit as the congregation sustains their applause. The two men embrace once more. This time when they separate, they smile knowingly at each other before Bart quickly makes his way offstage.

Luke motions toward Bart as he loudly addresses the applauding congregation, "My brother, Pastor Bart Baxter! *A Very Special Man!*"

The congregation strengthens their applause as parishioners nod to one another in agreement.

Luke lowers his eyes and shifts them side-to-side before he slides a fast one past the energized parishioners.

"Before we leave today we'd like to *take the offering…*"

* * *

Eleven-fifteen in the church parking lot as a hot sun burns away puddles that remain from this morning's surprise rain shower. A decade's worth of Sundays would see this parking lot emptied already, but today it's abuzz with chatter and excitement at the handsome, charismatic Pastor Bart Baxter. An animated Mrs Grace Evans spins tales of Pastor Bart as a toddler to younger parishioners as a small circle of teenage girls discuss him privately.

"I think he has a cute butt!" one girl confides discreetly.

A jokester girl whispers, "Imagine *Pastor Luke's butt!*"

The circle of girls hums in reply, *"Ewwwww!"*

Above the parking lot, mini blinds slowly open in a second-story window.

"Well there's no denying that you've sparked something here Bart," Luke says while looking out the window.

Bart's relaxing on an old fabric couch that's faded to gray. "I told you Luke, I've been reborn—"

Luke laughs.

"—and soon everyone will suffer the consequences."

Smiling, Luke looks down at a tabulation of the day's offerings. "Well the consequence of today is we pulled in twice what we normally get, and that's not counting the tithes yet."

Bart wags his finger knowingly at Luke, "Ah, you see Luke? Those cheap bastards want to come in here to gossip with their friends and get a free motivational speech from you every Sunday, all while they're sitting firmly on their wallets. I gave them a little show today and suddenly they have money to give."

Luke listens as Bart continues.

"Today was just a taste of what's in store for this church, Luke. We're gonna get you outta that dusty old suit and into something silky, and *we're gonna bring in a band.*"

Luke looks down at his sportcoat-and-slacks combo and flaps the lapels. He loves it.

"There's nothing wrong with this suit Bart! It fits me like a glove."

Bart laughs as he attempts to talk sense into his brother, "You're packed into it like a sausage—*I can see your balls man!*"

Luke looks down at his crotch.

"Nah that's normal, that's how it's supposed to fit."

Bart shakes his head emphatically as Luke changes the subject.

"Alright well we don't have any money for a band but some of the kids in our Youth Group might play instruments. I think Jimmy Edwards plays some type of horn?"

Luke looks deep into his own head as he tries to identify the specific horn played by Jimmy Edwards.

Bart's voice puts an end to the thought. "No, no kids. No hacks. We need real players. Guys with style and groove."

Luke sighs, then sighs again as he gives in to Bart's request. "Yeah okay, I'll put an ad out but I can't promise anything. The church just doesn't have much money to bring on new stuff like this, Bart."

Bart reassures his brother, "You bring that groove band in and you won't be worrying about money much longer, Luke. *Trust me.*"

DIFFERENT HUES OF RED

For the first time in months, the church sign has something new to say:

See our New Praise Band at Tomorrow Morning's Sunday Service 10am.

Signs of life emanate from within the church. A guitar is tuned. Cymbals, gently tapped, ring at different pitches. An electric bass burps notes to a musical scale.

Inside, the band prepares to audition. A smiling man in his sixties wears tinted glasses, a guitar and a bowling shirt embroidered with the name Pops. A mid-30s stoner jokes to himself as he adjusts his drum kit and laughs. To his left, an exceedingly creepy man in his late-40s scowls at his amp while plinking a few sinister notes on his bass. He's totally bald on top and has white tufts of hair on the sides of his head, similar in appearance to *Captain Stubing* of *Love Boat* fame. The church's very own in-house Organist maintains her esteemed position at the organ; she's ready to rock.

Fronting the band is a rotund dark-haired man in his 40s named Donny. The big man is light on his feet as he deftly darts around the stage making sure all the musicians have a copy of the setlist.

Luke and Bart sit together in the center of the second pew. Bart's arms are crossed in disappointment.

"This is the band you got?"

"It's the best I could do with the money we have," Luke says. "These guys work cheap and the big guy Donny says he's played with them all and they're solid."

Bart can't help but notice the creepy elephant in the room. He leans over to Luke and whispers, "Look at the bass player."

The bass player continues to scowl heavily while tuning his bass.

"The guy looks like a serial killer."

Luke whispers back, "No no he's good, Donny said they're all good."

Donny has finished distributing the setlist and grabs his microphone. He coughs once off-mic then looks over nervously at Luke and Bart.

"Okay Pastors, we're ready if you're ready?"

Luke and Bart nod.

Donny counts the band in; they hit their marks perfectly and begin playing an upbeat, groovy gospel song. The Organist holds her own as the big man bounces to the rhythm and starts singing in a beautifully sweet tenor voice.

Surprised, Bart leans over to Luke and yells over the music, "They're not exactly what I had in mind Luke but they're good!"

Luke yells back, "See I told you! You gotta listen to your big brother sometimes Bart!"

The song continues as Bart and Luke enjoy the performance.

Bart makes a request, "Do you think we could get them color-coordinated for tomorrow's service?"

Dismayed, Luke replies, "Well I'm not a miracle worker here Bart but I'll ask."

Bart drinks in the music. There's no doubt they can groove.

"Yeah they are pretty good," Bart openly admits.

Luke overhears Bart and smiles.

As the band continues playing, the brothers nod their heads to the groove.

* * *

A cheery new sun broadcasts an exciting message from the Salvation Alley church sign:

> *Join us for the debut of our new Praise Band today at 10am.*
> *Extra seating available!*

It's 9 a.m. by the church clock as the band is busy setting up their equipment. *Technically speaking,* the band is color-coordinated. In plain text, however, each member wears clothing in a different hue of red. The permanently scowling bass player wears a light pink dress-shirt that's open at the collar. To his right, the Stoner Drummer is clad in a reddish-brown long-sleeved shirt with a surf logo on the breast pocket. On the other side of the drummer sits the guitarist, Pops, wearing contentment on his face to complement the cherry red corduroy dress shirt he's tucked into brown slacks. Singer Donny cuts a massive figure in his full suit, complete with vest, in rich burgundy. The Organist rounds out the ensemble in a dark red formal gown.

Bart walks in the front door of the church and immediately notices the band's color mismatch. He bites his lip as he approaches the band on stage.

"Hey you guys look great!"

Everyone in the band smiles and acknowledges the compliment except the bass player, who just glares at Bart.

Donny stops what he's doing and approaches Bart with an outstretched hand. "Hello Pastor Baxter, I don't think we've been formally introduced. I'm Donny Davis."

The two men shake hands as Bart politely instructs, "Please Donny, call me Bart."

"Okay *Bart,*" Donny says with a warm smile, happy that he's already hitting it off with Pastor Baxter. "I have today's setlist here if you and Pastor Luke would like to review it?"

Donny offers the setlist to Bart but he declines.

"I don't need to see it, I trust you Donny. The band's your area of *expertise* and I don't wanna step on it. As long as you're playing something really uplifting and groovy, Pastor Luke and I are good with it."

Donny beams at the compliment, "Yes of course Pastor Baxt—"

Bart catches Donny with a friendly raise of the eyebrow.

"I mean Bart," Donny says with an aw-shucks grin.

The men share a friendly smile—only Donny's is genuine.

Bart motions Donny over to the side of the stage, away from the band, for a private discussion. The two men huddle up.

"So Donny," Bart says in a voice just above a whisper, "I'm going to join you guys at the end of the set today to sing a song."

Donny matches Bart's whispery tone, "Okay what song?"

"I'm not gonna tell you guys yet. I want it to be a big surprise for everyone."

Donny's eyes flash and his chubby face dimples, "Oooh, *exciting!*" Donny loves surprises.

Bart continues quietly, "I just need you to add some tender highlights in the background as I lead. Good?"

"Great!" Donny quietly exclaims.

Bart glances over at the bassist, currently busy adjusting his amp and wearing a scowl. He drops his voice to a whisper, "Hey so what's with the bass player?"

Donny looks over his shoulder toward the band area then whispers back to Bart, "Oh that's Joey."

Donny leans in close to Bart and lowers his whispered-voice even further.

"He's a little different but don't worry," Donny looks reassuringly at Bart, *"I can control him."*

Bart's eyebrows narrow as he blinks blankly at Donny. He's not sure what that means, but it doesn't sound good.

Donny notices Bart's unease and whispers an explanation, "Good bass players are *really hard to find."*

Luke surprises the men as he loudly interrupts, "So are we ready for today?"

"Yes indeed we are Pastor Luke," Donny replies confidently. "Me and *Bart...*"

Donny draws the name out as he looks to Bart for approval. Bart nods him on.

"...just went over the setlist and it looks like we're a go!"

Luke looks strangely preoccupied but musters some unenthused praise for the big man, "Great Donny."

Donny smiles proudly as Bart bites the inside of his cheek. Donny's innocence is almost too much for him to stomach.

Luke diverts his attention to Bart. "Pastor Bart, would you join me in the office so we can go over the sermon?" Luke sounds tired.

"Sure Pastor Luke!" Bart's sarcasm flies over Donny's naïve head.

The two men retreat offstage as Donny readies a second microphone for Bart.

* * *

"So shall we go over those sermon notes, Pastor Luke?"

Bart, last to enter the room, shuts the office door. He notices Luke becoming very nervous.

"Luke, what's up man?"

Luke is so emotional he can't find the words to speak. Bart is worried.

"Luke man," Bart softens his voice, "are you alright?"

Luke finally speaks. "I can't do this anymore Bart."

Bart looks at him curiously, "What the music thing? We can slow down man if it'll make you feel—"

"No, not the music thing. I mean the church. *All of it.* I can't do it anymore."

Bart takes a concerned seat on the couch as Luke pulls the blinds up and gazes out the window at nothing in particular. The beauty of the day goes unnoticed.

"You know I never wanted to do this Bart," Luke confides.

Bart looks sympathetically at his brother as Luke bares his soul to him.

"Dad always wanted one of us to take over the church and I'm the oldest and, you know, you had your own thing going on so it all just sorta got handed to me. And what was I going to do, *say no?*"

Bart understands. Being the son of a pastor, especially the oldest son, can be a blessing or a curse depending on your life's ambition.

"So I inherited this big pain in the ass from dad. A small church with no future."

Luke's gaze falls on a pigeon perched on a wire overlooking the parking lot. On a day bursting with sunshine, the bird looks inexcusably lonely.

"I have people here who look to me for all the answers. Well, I don't have the answers, Bart. *I don't even like the people who ask me for them.*"

Bart laughs softly.

"I'm just not cutout to be a Pastor, Bart. I can think of ten different places I'd rather be on Sunday morning than here in this church."

Luke turns away from the window and looks to Bart. Tears of despair have moistened his eyes.

"What do I do, Bart?"

Bart pulls at his chin as he thinks for a few seconds. He holds up his hand, instructing Luke to put his tears on hold while he completes his thought.

Bart finishes his thought. He looks decisively at Luke.

"This is what you're gonna do…"

* * *

Ten minutes prior to the service and the congregation has nearly doubled in size since Pastor Bart Baxter was unveiled. Seats remain vacant, however; of two hundred available seats, roughly a hundred remain.

Bart is again schmoozing with the congregation. A line of people stretches up the aisle waiting to shake his hand. *Waiting to touch him.*

From his position near the stage, Bart notices an elderly lady walk in the door. On this warm sunny day, she wears a peacoat and two thick scarves wrapped tightly around her neck and receives immediate attention from older parishioners. She looks vaguely familiar, then Bart overhears her name spoken: It's Grace Christianson, apparently recovered from the chill afflicting her last week. *The Money Train has arrived.*

Bart politely breaks from the handshake line, "I'm sorry can you please excuse me for one second? Mrs Christianson is here and I'd like to help her to her seat."

An aisle filled with sweaty palms watches in unison as Bart glides past them toward Mrs Christianson.

"Ahh Mrs Christianson it is so nice to see you again." Bart reaches his hands out courteously to her. "Are you feeling better this week?"

Mrs Christianson latches onto Bart's outstretched hands. Her hands are ice cold. "Oh thank you Pastor *Luke,* it's just been so durned cold this week!"

Bart ignores the incorrect name like a pro. "Well I'll have you know this *entire congregation* prayed for your warmth over the last week."

"Oh thank you so much Pastor Luke," Mrs Christianson's voice turns chipper, "and it worked! Say, how's your wife?"

Mrs Christianson's confusion is really keeping Bart on his toes here. "Oh she's just fine…" Bart quickly searches for something more to say.

"She felt that chill last week too!"

"Oh didn't we all!" Mrs Christianson happily laments, grateful that someone else understands the pain she endured during last week's cold spell. Nights reached as low as the *mid-60s.*

Bart and Mrs Christianson share a warm laugh.

"Say Pastor Luke, did you do something with your hair?"

Bart suddenly has a strange hallucination. Inhabiting Luke's body, he speaks to Bart's unshaven and sickly doppelganger while a completely bald Mrs Christianson wields an energized cattle-prod and maniacally chews gum next to Bart's double. As the bald Mrs Christianson zaps at the air near the doppelganger, Bart, in Luke's body, suddenly realizes that *he is bald too. Horrifying.*

Without missing a beat, Bart's focus returns to the here-and-now. "Well, um, yes!" Bart stammers toward the answer, "I—I grew it out!"

Mrs Christianson smiles and clicks her tongue. "I knew something looked different about you Pastor Luke!"

Bart is growing nervous, unsure how long he can keep this up. He preempts Mrs Christianson before she makes another move in confusion-checkers. "May I take you to your seat Mrs Christianson?"

Grace Christianson delights at the offer. "Oh sure, it's right down there next to Grace Evans!"

Bart offers an arm to Mrs Christianson, "Okay hold on to my arm and watch your step dear lady!"

Mrs Christianson loves the attention and happily hooks onto Bart's arm for the trip down the aisle.

In full view of a congregation whose esteem for him only grows, Bart navigates down the congested aisle and arrives at Mrs Christianson's pew. Mrs Evans, herself also wearing a thick scarf, is already seated next to Mrs Christianson's empty seat.

Bart hands Mrs Christianson off at her pew. "Okay Mrs Christianson, enjoy the sermon and please *stay warm!*"

"Oh I will. It's been so durned cold!"

Bart smiles as he checks his watch. He waves off the sweaty palms still waiting for him in the aisle as he retreats back to the offstage area. The sweaty palms smile to each other as they find their seats.

Meanwhile, Mrs Christianson and Mrs Evans exchange simultaneous hellos.

"Oh hi *Grace* how've you been?"

* * *

Music fills the warm air outside Salvation Alley as the sun arcs through the sky. It's 10:50 a.m. and the band is wrapping up the last song in their setlist. The congregation is lively and smiling as Donny looks toward the far side of the stage and nods. Donny motions to the band to bring the volume down as Bart enters the stage. The congregation *oohs* and *ahhs* as Pastor Bart grabs the second microphone.

Bart speaks a song title off-mic toward Donny and the band, "*The Old Rugged Cross.*"

Donny's eyes widen as he shakes his head in amazement at the selection. It's a beautiful song choice that gives Donny the chills.

He confesses to Bart off-mic, *"Goosepimples* Pastor Bart." Donny pulls at his skin to illustrate as a shivery wave runs uncontrolled down his big, burgundy-suited body.

Bart gives a solemn nod to Donny and the band.

Pops and the Organist smile broadly at the song selection while Joey, buried in the back next to the Stoner Drummer, just scowls in Bart's general direction. Donny turns back to the band and counts them in. They hit their marks perfectly as Bart begins singing.

"On a hill far away, stood an old rugged Cross..."

Moans of Christian ecstasy hail from the congregation as people stare in awe at Pastor Bart.

"The emblem of suffering and shame..."

Per Pastor Bart's preservice request, Donny adds soft vocal highlights as Bart continues singing.

"And I love that old Cross where the dearest and best..."

Contagious tears flow openly in the congregation.

"For a world of lost sinners was slain..."

Bart gently speaks into the microphone, "Donny, would you mind taking over while I address our brothers and sisters?"

Donny immediately takes the song back up, singing softly in his beautiful tenor voice, *"So I'll cherish the old rugged Cross..."*

Bart addresses the church as Donny sings eggshell-delicate in the background.

"Brothers and sisters of the church..."

The congregation leans forward as one to listen to Pastor Bart.

"I'd like to call my brother Pastor Luke up to make an announcement."

Luke rises from his seat in the front pew and walks shakily to the pulpit as the congregation sits on pins and needles. Luke and Bart embrace. In their embrace, Bart hears Luke crying. Bart feels his own eyes become teary but he maintains his composure.

After the brothers' release their embrace, Luke mans the pulpit while Bart takes position on his flank.

Donny's voice floats ghostlike in the air, *"And exchange it some day for a crown..."*

Pastor Luke addresses his congregation. "Brothers, sisters...The Lord has brought a new challenge to my life..."

Bart bows his head as Luke continues speaking.

"And with that challenge comes some health concerns that might limit my ability to serve this wonderful *flock...*"

Bart's bowed head cocks ever-so-slightly at the odd word choice as gasps are heard from the congregation.

Donny's voice fills the emptiness, *"For the dear Lamb of God..."*

"Because of this new challenge, I am appointing my brother—this *good man* right here," Luke reaches back to put an arm around Bart's shoulder, "as the new Head Pastor of Salvation Alley Church."

Shock, sadness and excitement pulse through the congregation all at once.

Recognizing the serious nature of Pastor Luke's announcement, Donny ceases singing and instead hums softly into the microphone. Donny's a real pro.

"Pastor Bart if you will, please address the church."

Silence from the pews as Bart and Luke exchange positions at the pulpit.

Bart speaks, "Church, it is my great honor to accept this hallowed position as Head Pastor. I truly believe that the Lord has a plan for all of us here."

Bart pauses.

"Together, *strong,* and with the guiding hand of God, we will go forth and *we will prosper."*

A few excited *Amens* ring out from the congregation as songbird Donny softly hums in the background.

"We've planned a Benefit Concert & Potluck for Pastor Luke here at the church this Saturday night—"

Excitement and cheers are heard in the pews. Luke laughs warmly and wipes tears from his eyes.

Bart raises his voice to be heard over the cheers for his brother, "And we hope to see you all there!"

The congregation rallies into applause for Pastor Luke and Pastor Bart.

"Pastor Luke and I are going to retreat to the office now to pray for one another. We ask that you pray for us this week as we make this transition whole."

The congregation responds with a shout, "Yes!"

Bart's humility changes to defiance as he speaks his final words to the congregation. "I can assure this congregation of one thing. In God's holy name, Pastor Luke, myself and *this magnificent congregation* will fight together as one!"

The congregation roars their support as tears flow.

Bart loudly commands, "Ushers, take the offering! And Donny and the band…" Bart turns toward them. Donny has never been more focused in his life.

"Play us out!"

On command, Donny tears into a verse of "The Old Rugged Cross".

"Then He'll call me some day to my home far away…"

Luke and Bart place arms over each other's shoulders and walk offstage as purses and wallets are emptied into offering baskets.

GOODBYE

Saturday night and the parking lot of Salvation Alley is packed tight with cars, including the old dust-caked Datsun. From inside the church we hear Donny's voice singing to the world within. Outside, the church sign sings to the world without:

> *Pastor Luke Baxter Benefit Concert and Potluck Tonight 6pm!*

Inside, a mammothly tuxed Donny grinds down on a low note while the band plays behind him. The congregation mingles in the pews, in the aisles, and at tables full of food erected along a side wall. A large box near the front of the stage, directly in front of Donny, is labeled *Donations for Pastor Luke*. Envelopes are routinely dropped inside the box by parishioners both coming and going. Luke and Bart helm the potluck table; Luke holds a gigantic plastic spoon while Bart wields an even larger pair of salad tongs. Happiness permeates the church.

Mrs Christianson appears at an aisle entrance, struggling under the weight of an enormous party cake that bears a message written in frosting, *"Goodbye Pastor Luke"*. The two snugly wrapped scarves haven't left her neck all week and she now has the tail end of one scarf wrapped around her mouth and nose. Luke and Bart quickly abandon their posts to tend to Mrs Christianson and her colossal cake. Luke is first on-scene.

"Oh please Mrs Christianson let me get that for you!" Luke takes the cake from Mrs Christianson as Bart arrives.

Bart offers kind words to Mrs Christianson. "It's beautiful Mrs Christianson! And thank you so much for coming!"

A frigid Mrs Christianson shudders in disbelief, "It's just so durned cold out!"

Bart performs a quick survey of the congregation's attire: none wear jackets, some wear shorts.

Confused, Mrs Christianson leans in toward Bart and points at Luke suspiciously. "Who's that?" she whispers.

Bart looks at Luke, who is transporting the cake bearing his name to the potluck table. Here we go again.

"Oh that is...my brother, Mrs Christianson. He's a good man."

Mrs Christianson stares suspiciously at Luke then looks back to Bart, who gives her a nod of approval. She nods at Bart's endorsement of the stranger carrying her cake.

Luke arrives at the potluck table with the gargantuan cake and quickly begins cutting it into pieces while the band plays into the night.

* * *

In the light of a full moon, only two cars are seen in the church parking lot: A mid-90s Oldsmobile Cutlass Ciera in blue and the ancient Datsun in dust. Pops, the praise band's ever-smiling guitarist, walks toward the Oldsmobile with his guitar case slung over his shoulder. In his hands he carries a heavily laden paper plate wrapped with tinfoil. Parked across the street from him, under a streetlamp, is a black van with a large, black-tinted side window.

From inside the van, a smooth, hairless hand gently parts dark curtains hanging within. The cuff of a light-pink dress shirt, buttoned tight at the wrist, is barely visible in the darkness of the van. Through the black-tinted window, the occupant views Pops at his Oldsmobile. Pops places the paper plate on top of his car, opens the trunk, and places his guitar case inside.

At the Oldsmobile, Pops hums to himself as he removes the tinfoil from his plate to reveal a huge chunk of frosted cake. He grabs the chunk and inserts it whole into his mouth. Pops continues humming as he chews down the cake. Behind Pops, across the street, the van and its occupant lurk ominously.

From the van's tinted side window, Pops is observed chewing and ultimately swallowing his cake. He enters his car, starts it, and slowly exits the parking lot. As Pops drives past the van, the smooth-handed occupant closes the curtains and lights a cigarette. In the utter blackness of the van, the cigarette burns red.

A red dome-light clicks on in the van to reveal Joey, the creepy, scowling praise band bassist. The van's main cabin is curtained off from the front seats. Curtains also cover the rear door windows. Joey, scowling, sits comfortably in a high-backed office chair, smoking a cigarette and sharpening a large hunting knife. A vast collection of knives, bathed in red by the dome-light, hang from every available inch of cabin space. On the floor, near the rear doors, lies his bass guitar case.

The Gift That Keeps On Giving

A handful of kids rush to class at Millard Filmore Elementary as a faded yellow '77 Datsun drops disheveled fifth-grader Bart Baxter off in front of the school.

From inside the vehicle Bart's father, Pastor James Baxter, yells to him, "Bartholomew did you pack your Bible?!"

Bart cringes. Not only is his dad drawing attention by *yelling*, he's also using the name Bart hates *and* he's referencing his Bible. That's three strikes before Bart even has a chance to swing.

"Yeah dad I got it!"

Mr Baxter yells again, "Okay son have a good day! *I love you!*"

Mr Baxter's car backfires and pulls away with a squealing timing belt. It doesn't get much worse as a kid.

With only a few minutes before class begins, Bart rushes toward his building. Manning the doors are the inseparable bullies Jerry and Larry. Blonde-haired, overweight and having an intensely punchable face, Jerry is the fifth-grade's class bully. His deputy is the big toothed, beady eyed, diminutive Larry. Larry's eyes look like someone placed tiny black marbles in the sockets where his orbs should be. Jerry is the coolest kid Larry's ever known and his allegiance to him was sworn years ago. To be precise, it was pledged in the second-grade after Jerry dunked his head in a toilet.

After hearing the exchange between Bart and his father, the pair jumps at their chance to needle Bart. Jerry starts in, *"Bartholomew* did you pack your Bible!?"

Larry joins the hunt. "Ha-ha-ha *Bartholomew!* Pack your Bible and your applesauce *Bartholomew!* I love you!"

Fifth-grader Julie, dropped off moments after her friend Bart, rushes after him toward the building they both share. She catches up to him just as Larry and Jerry are starting in. Julie isn't afraid of the doofus twins and she won't stand for them giving Bart a hard time. He's like a kid brother to her.

"Why don't you guys just shut up and stop being so mean all the time!"

Jerry whines out a response, "Why don't you make me Julie?"

Loyal lackey Larry joins the fray. "Yeah why don't you make us Julie?"

"How about I kick you in the nards and make you cry in front of your boyfriend again?"

Jerry gulps as Larry looks away in shame for his leader.

Mission accomplished, Julie leads a now-grinning Bart through the doors and into the building. As the doors close, Jerry calls for and receives a jumping high-five from Larry.

* * *

It's just before ten in Ms Pilbert's fifth-grade class and the rowdy kids have had too much sugar this morning. They're busy answering Ms Pilbert's *Big Question of the Day.* Up next is Jerry.

"And what do you want to be when you grow up, Jerry?" Ms Pilbert asks.

"I want to be the President so I can drop rockets from my big ol' bomber jet on the Russians!"

Larry is ecstatic, "That's so cool Jerry can I be President with you!?"

Jerry makes a jet with his hand and flies it on a bombing run over his desk. Through puckered lips, sound effects are added.

"SHEE-eew!"

Jerry's jet loops up high over the desk then circles around for another pass. The Russians don't stand a chance.

"Boom! Boom! BAAM!"

Larry wants in on the action. He purses his lips and flies a hand over Jerry's desk, "SHEE-eew!"

President Jerry pushes Larry's hand away from the desk and out of his airspace as he gives him a stern dressing down, "Stop Larry I'm not done yet!"

Larry straightens up and holds his jet-hand motionless over his desk, beady eyes fixed firmly on Jerry as he awaits orders.

The thought of President Jerry makes Ms Pilbert nauseous but she squeaks out a positive comment for Jerry's sake. "That's good Jerry and I think you'd make a great President."

Jerry now adds machine-gun strafing to his bombing run, "Choo-Choo-Choo-Choo-Choo!" Spit flies and froths on Jerry's puckered lips as Larry continues waiting patiently for the President's go-order.

"Boom-Boom-BAAM!"

Ms Pilbert turns her attention to quiet, polite Bart Baxter. The yin to Jerry's yang.

"Okay Bart, your turn. What do you want to be when you grow up?"

Upon hearing Bart's name, Jerry immediately ends his bombing mission and looks up. Larry's gaze remains fixed on the awesomeness that is Jerry, jet hand still hovering motionless over the battlefield.

"His name's not Bart it's *Bar-tho-lo-mew.*" Jerry intentionally over-pronounces Bart's name.

Larry drops his hand and joins forces with Jerry. "Ha-ha yeah *Bar-tho-lo-mew!*"

Jerry and Larry take turns overpronouncing Bart's proper name while the class giggles.

Ms Pilbert didn't like Jerry the moment he walked into her classroom this year. If she was his age, she'd kick him and his marble-eyed twerp friend Larry right in their little nuts. She scolds them both, "Boys, enough! It's Bart's turn to talk."

Ms Pilbert shifts back to Bart. "Bart? What do you want to be when you grow up sweetie?"

Jerry just can't help himself. "A Farter! Bart the Farter!"

The class laughs. Larry's hacking laugh trumps them all.

Ms Pilbert's tired of the interruptions and darts a firm glare at Jerry, "Jerry, enough! You two stop it or you're going to the Principal's office."

The class hums, *"Ooooohh!"*

"Now hush it, I'm talking to Far—"giggles are suppressed in the classroom as Ms Pilbert catches herself"—I mean Bart!"

Satisfied that she's regained control from the bullies, Ms Pilbert finally gets back to Bart and prompts him again.

"Bart?"

Bart replies meekly, "I want to be a businessman."

Ms Pilbert is encouraged by Bart's response. "Wow, that's an interesting job Bart! Why do you want to be a businessman?"

Matter-of-factly and with a child's logic, Bart replies, "So I can have lots of money and nobody will ever make fun of me again."

Ms Pilbert is struck by the honesty in Bart's response.

"Hey businessman can you sell me some *farts!*" It's Jerry being obnoxious again.

Larry cackles and jumps in, "Yeah that's good Jerry! Bart, Fart! Bart the Farter ha-ha!"

Jerry and Larry make fart sounds and laugh hysterically at each other while Bart stares through the classroom window toward the horizon. In the distance, standing above the trees and buildings, is an ornate church steeple with a cross on top. In the late-morning sun, the cross twinkles like a diamond. Bart tunes-out the class shenanigans; he's hypnotized by that twinkling cross and the promise it holds for him.

As the distant church bell tolls ten, Jerry and Larry continue their disruption. Jerry leads as usual. "Fart face ha-ha-ha! Bart's face is a fart face!"

Larry piles on, "Can I fart on your face Bart?! I promise there won't be *poop!*"

The entire class laughs hysterically as Bart gazes out toward his glittering diamond.

* * *

A dull cross is weakly backlit next to a familiar church sign that boringly reads:

Salvation Alley Pastor James Baxter

It's 6:15 p.m. on a moonless Sunday night, two days after Bart's tumultuous school day, and churchgoers are already seated and listening to Pastor Baxter's monotone delivery of the latest church news. Bart sits in the first pew, an empty seat next to him where older brother Luke would be if he wasn't home sick.

Outside, graffiti mars one wall of the church. Near the parking lot entrance, a shadowy figure loiters near a tree. As a shiny new Cadillac slowly pulls into the lot, the headlights illuminate the shadowy figure to reveal a homeless man urinating on a tree. The Cadillac pulls into a front parking space marked *Guest.* The driver exits the vehicle slowly, surely. A tall black man, dressed impeccably in a white suit with matching fedora, struts casually toward the church's rear entrance while gripping a Bible between his thumb and fingers.

Inside, an offering is being taken as the organist plays softly. Pastor James Baxter gently paces the stage and swings his arms from the elbows down, his preferred method of dance. Bart yawns from the front row. As offering baskets are passed down each row, mothers hand quarters to their children to drop inside. A few people place dollars in the basket, while a mischievous teenager drops gum inside and giggles to herself. As the baskets boomerang back from the final row, the ushers gather them and retreat to the counting room.

Pastor James Baxter addresses the congregation, *"Isn't God grand?"*

"Amen!" replies the congregation.

Pastor Baxter continues, "As you may have heard, I've invited a special guest tonight to deliver the Lord's message to us. I have not heard this man's message yet, so I'm excited to say that we all get to hear it for the first time tonight, *together."* Pastor Baxter smiles warmly at his congregation.

"I'm confident you will enjoy the message tonight and, most importantly," Pastor Baxter glances over at his yawning son Bart, "find meaning in it."

"Our guest has a style all his own and I would like you all to give a warm Salvation Alley welcome to Bishop Ronny Patterson!"

The congregation applauds lightly as Pastor James Baxter exits the stage.

Suddenly, the lights go out in the church. The congregation gasps and murmurs. A baby cries loudly.

A spotlight snaps on, illuminating the immaculately dressed Bishop Ronny Patterson. His legs are spread to shoulder width, hands clasped in front of him at waist level, head bowed. The congregation quickly hushes.

Bishop Ronny's left arm quickly lifts as he snaps his finger into a point toward the balcony. With the snap, a funky gospel song begins. Bishop Ronny begins dancing and encouraging the congregation to clap their hands in time with the music.

"Come on baby clap those hands! Jesus is in the house!"

The song is so catchy, half of the congregation immediately complies. Bishop Ronny works the crowd heavily, employing every dance move in the book: the Electric Slide, a few Pop-and-Locks and even a Typewriter jittering spectacularly across the stage.

"Brothers and sisters let's get up on our feet! Come on, *get on up!*"

Bishop Ronny catches on like wildfire. Everyone is on their feet except for a few elderly folks with walkers.

"Whoa-whoa-whoaaaaa! Young lady, young man, you can do it mama let's stand!"

Bishop Ronny moonwalks back toward an elderly lady seated next to her walker. She's smiling, clapping, and moving to the music but she lacks the confidence to stand. Bishop Ronny gently helps her up and gets her standing with her walker.

"We celebratin' Jesus tonight! We're not stoppin' until Jesus tells us to stop! *Come on!*"

The entire congregation is now on their feet and clapping as one. Bishop Ronny descended on this church like Manna from Heaven and they're eating him up.

From the front row, young Bart excitedly raises his fists to the sky and screams out, *"Hallelujah!"*

Noticing Bart's outburst, Bishop Ronny breakdances into an Arm Wave and ends it with a smiling point at Bart.

The previously crying baby now laughs in his mother's swaying arms as Bishop Ronny hits the splits on stage.

Outside, the urinating homeless man crouches in the dark with his pants down.

* * *

A satisfied, exhausted congregation listens to Bishop Ronny Patterson bid farewell as their stomachs flutter with delight.

"I'm so thankful that the Lord brought us all together tonight to experience His divine energy. Next week I'm heading overseas for missionary work but I hope in a few years we'll meet again when God feels the time is right."

Many in the congregation are visibly saddened that they won't see Bishop Ronny again. Little do they know that *missionary work* in Bishop Ronny parlance translates to *golfing in the Bahamas.*

"Thank you and God bless. I'll hand the reins back over to Pastor Baxter now."

The congregation thunders with applause and cheering for Bishop Ronny as an ecstatic Pastor Baxter approaches him near the pulpit. Bishop Ronny hands the mic over to Pastor Baxter, who accepts it and shakes Bishop Ronny's hand with two of his own.

Pastor Baxter leans closer to a widely smiling Bishop Ronny and speaks to him off-mic, "That was beautiful Bishop Ronny, thank you!"

Through his smile Bishop Ronny gives a stern reminder to Pastor Baxter, "Don't you forget my offerin' now."

Pastor Baxter nods happily to Bishop Ronny.

The congregation continues applauding Bishop Ronny as he quickly makes his way offstage. Pastor Baxter mans the pulpit with a warm smile.

"Thank you Bishop Ronny! We'd like to take a special offering now for the Bishop as he goes away on missionary duty—"

Purses fly open and fists hold wads of cash high in the air, ready for Bishop Ronny's special offering.

* * *

Bishop Ronny Patterson's Cadillac slowly pulls out of the parking lot as a smiling Pastor James Baxter stands watching with his son. The Cadillac drives away. Bart looks up at his dad and notices tears falling from his eyes.

"Why're you crying dad?"

Pastor James Baxter doesn't know how to explain church business to his son. He opts for the white lie. "I'm just happy son. I'm happy that everyone here tonight was happy."

Young Bart furrows his brow in confusion.

* * *

Tuesday morning, 3 a.m. Bart and Julie are both asleep in bed. Bart awakens from his dream and shoots straight up, rubbing his face as he tries to recall fleeting details from it. Julie continues sleeping next to him as Bart tries hard to remember.

Bart looks at Julie, still asleep. "Julie…we have to get married," he says.

Busy enjoying her own dream, Julie consents in absentia. "Mm-hmm," she coos.

Bart watches Julie as she slumbers peacefully. He gently caresses her face before going back to sleep.

* * *

Tuesday morning, 8 a.m. Julie cleans dishes as Bart eats toast, drinks coffee and flips through the newspaper to the Local News section. He spots an interesting headline:

Los Angeles Evangelist Starts National Religious Broadcast Network

Accompanying the article is a picture of a smiling, older black man. It's a much older Bishop Ronny Patterson, with the caption:

Bishop Ronald Patterson set to launch Blessed Flock Network

Below and to the right of the article is a separate headline:

Silky Strangler Strikes Again

The first line of the strangler article reads:

"The killer identified by one lucky survivor as 'A man with very smooth hands' has struck again, this time in…"

The remaining text falls out of view. A crude sketch is shown of the strangler, essentially just a scowling white man wearing a baseball cap with hair spilling out over his ears. It vaguely resembles praise band bassist Joey, except that Joey is bald. Of course, hat-wearing men are frequently *hiding their baldness.*

Bart exclaims, "Oh shit look, it's Bishop Ronny!" Bart laughs excitedly but Julie has no idea who he's talking about.

"Oh is that one of your sleazy Preacher buddies?"

Bart is very excited. "No no, Julie check it out—I was just thinking about this guy!"

Julie sees Bart's enthusiasm and plays along. "Okay, so what about him?"

"This guy came to my dad's church once way back in the 80s and blew the lid off the place!"

Julie rolls her eyes but Bart presses on.

"Julie, you don't understand. My dad wanted to mix things up a bit to get more money coming into the church so he invited this guy in one night to see if he could get things moving. Nobody knew who he was, he just showed up and my dad vouched for him."

"Hmm sounds familiar doesn't it," Julie raises her eyebrows, *"Pastor Bart?"* Julie never fails to see things that others don't.

Bart pauses to consider Julie's observation.

Julie gets him back on track, "And?"

Bart resumes his story, *"And* he killed it! The whole congregation was ready to riot." Bart offers his own firsthand account. "Julie, I was there and *I* was ready to riot."

Unimpressed, Julie asks, "Okay...and did it work?"

In his excitement, Bart forgot the point of his own story. "Did what work?"

"Did it bring more money into the church?"

Bart looks dismayed, "Well, yes and no."

Julie raises her eyebrows again—Bart's just too easy to read.

Bart explains, "He took seven hundred bucks that night in a special offering. My dad took seventy-three fifty." Bart saddens at the thought.

"Dad never told me but I overheard him telling my mom later that night."

"Well that sucks, Bart."

Bart nods his head in agreement with Julie. "And what's worse is that the money everyone gave to Bishop Ronny meant they had even less to give my dad the following week."

Julie emits a meaty *harrumph* at the result of Bishop Ronny's visit.

Bart adds, "Bishop Ronny was the gift that kept on giving."

"And yet you like this guy!?"

Bart doesn't need time to think up a response. He implicitly understands Bishop Ronny.

"Julie, Bishop Ronny did things the right way. This church stuff is all a business. My dad never understood that but Bishop Ronny knew. It's showbusiness. Entertain people, make them feel good about themselves, then take their money for your efforts."

Julie's quick to respond, "Kinda like what you do!"

Bart laughs at Julie's observation. "No Julie not kinda—it's *exactly* what I do."

Julie laughs as Bart puts down the paper and approaches her.

"And it's what I will continue doing until I have everything I want, *and more.*" Bart kisses a receptive Julie.

Bart's cellphone suddenly rings in his pocket. Only one person besides Julie has his phone number. He pulls it out and answers it.

"Yeah Luke what's up?"

An inaudible voice is heard over the phone.

Bart looks discouraged, "Oh really?"

The inaudible voice continues talking.

Bart's discouragement immediately changes to surprise.

"Oh really!?" Bart perks up and laughs.

"Okay, let's plan on Saturday. Can you let the church know? Okay good."

Bart begins to hang up then pulls the phone back quickly, "Hey Luke wait! Let the church know about the first thing but not *the second thing.*"

Through the cellphone earpiece come the words, "Yeah, no shit."

"Okay, I was just making sure," replies Bart. He hangs up the phone and sits in stunned silence.

With concern painting her face, Julie inquires, "What happened?"

Bart stares at Julie in disbelief.

"The money train just reached its final stop."

The Money Train

The church sign has bad news today:

Please join us today at 11am to remember Grace Christianson. Burial follows.

With the service already begun, the parking lot is packed. A precious parking space is occupied by the obnoxious dust-caked Datsun.

Inside, flanking Mrs Christianson's open casket, are two separate easels. On one, a black-and-white picture of her on a yacht with a man a few inches shorter than herself, presumably Mr Christianson. On the other, a blown-up color photograph of old Mrs Christianson wearing a party hat, sunglasses and scarf, blowing out a single candle on a birthday cake.

To a packed house, Pastor Bart speaks fondly of Mrs Christianson.

"You know, Mrs Christianson came up to me a few weeks ago after the service. That dear little lady, she came up to me and she said, 'Pastor Bart, could ya' turn the heat up a little bit in the chapel? *It's just so durned cold in here.'*"

The congregation laughs warmly as Pastor Bart continues.

"And she said, 'You know Pastor Bart, this chapel of ours should really be bigger.' She says to me, 'Maybe you should think about building a *new church* because I think we've outgrown this one.'"

Bart pauses as a few heads nod from the pews.

"I says to Mrs Christianson, 'But Mrs Christianson, this church is our home. We like it here!' And Mrs Christianson, that dear lovely lady, she looked me square in the eye and she said, *'Well we'll like it there too*, Pastor Bart. We trust you and we'll go wherever you lead us.'"

Bart surveys the congregation. Many heads nod this time.

Bart raises his voice, "So today, to honor this wise woman…" Bart motions toward Mrs Christianson's open casket as the congregation becomes giddy with anticipation.

"I've decided that we all are going to find a new church…"

Excitement builds in the pews as Bart pours it on strong.

"A new home. A bigger home! To grow this congregation further in service to the Lord! To fulfill God's edict to us—to be fruitful and multiply!"

Shouts of *Amen* rain in from the congregation as Bart motions once again to Mrs Christianson's casket.

"And I assure you, *oh dear Mrs Christianson…"*

Bart pauses before delivering his final line.

"We *most certainly* will turn the heat up!"

Bart smiles out over his congregation. As excited praise and applause echoes throughout the church, Mrs Christianson lies still in her casket.

* * *

Luke, Bart and Julie are seated in Julie's small backyard patio discussing the day's events. Luke, wide-eyed and serious, is busy explaining something to Julie, who can't believe what she's hearing. Bart, still clothed in a suit, beams from ear-to-ear and nods along.

Julie replies to Luke, "So this lady left you a million dollars?"

Luke nods seriously then corrects Julie, "Well, she left *the church* a million dollars."

Bart can barely contain himself. He looks like he's about to burst into a thousand balloons full of glitter and butterflies.

"She doesn't have any family at all?" asks Julie.

Luke, still wide-eyed, silently shakes his head.

Bart finally speaks. "She named Pastor Luke Baxter as the executor of her will. The church got a million—everything else went to the American Legion."

"Wow." Julie is dumbfounded. She asks the obvious question, "So, uh, do the people in the church know this?"

Both Luke and Bart's lips tighten as they shake their heads in silence.

Julie explodes with laughter as the men shift uncomfortably in their seats.

Recovered from her laughing fit, Julie asks, "So what are you guys gonna do?"

Luke looks to Bart.

"Julie, my dear lady," Bart puffs his chest confidently, "we're going on television."

Julie is stunned. She looks at Luke, "Luke you can't let this knucklehead on TV they'll arrest him!"

Luke laughs loudly while Bart quietly tries to hush Julie.

"Whoa whoa easy there," Bart looks around nervously, "let's not throw around words like that!"

Julie and Luke both laugh hysterically while Bart adjusts his tie and composes himself.

"Julie baby," Bart adopts a mackdaddy tone, "I'm a businessman and *TV* is where the *money's at* in this business."

Luke responds by looking down at his hands while Julie watches Bart adjust his hair and suit in mock arrogance.

"Besides," Bart says, "some might say I was *made* for TV."

Julie and Luke look at Bart and nod in grudging acceptance—Bart is certainly made for TV.

Bart grabs Julie's hand and suddenly becomes very serious. "Hey Julie, there's something else I need to discuss with you."

Luke stands up, "Alright guys I think that's my cue to go."

Julie looks confused.

Bart, still holding Julie's hand, talks to Luke as he's leaving. "Alright Luke, don't forget I invited the network guy to watch our service tomorrow. He'll meet us in the office."

Luke looks less-than-thrilled, "Yeah, great. That guy's an asshole."

Luke begins making his way through the house as Bart yells to him, "Hey Luke come on, the guy was just trying to make some money."

"Yeah sure!" Luke shouts from inside the house.

Julie is still confused as to why Bart is holding her hand. Bart turns back and looks straight into her eyes.

"Julie?" Bart pauses as she returns his look. "We need to get married."

Julie's jaw hits the floor.

KINGS, QUEENS, BISHOPS & PAWNS

A gorgeous Southern California day is brewing as Julie's old Nissan Maxima sits in Sunday morning church traffic. Behind the wheel sits Bart, conversing with Julie in the passenger seat. Julie prefers not to drive if Bart is in the car; in her eyes, the only men being carted around by women are drunks and pimps.

"So you never thought I would propose to you?"

Julie looks at Bart and laughs. "Well I'm not sure if that was even a proposal. It felt more like a business transaction."

Bart laughs, "Well isn't that what marriage is?"

Julie gazes through the passenger window, thinking. Wondering.

"So you really want to do this?" she asks.

Bart grabs Julie's hand. She turns to look at him.

Bart's eyes empower his words, "Julie, you'll never have to work again."

Julie looks back through the window, attempting to foretell the future.

Bart speaks further, "A man of God—"

Julie interrupts him with a sarcastic laugh.

Ignoring Julie's sarcasm, Bart begins again. "Julie, a man of God has to be married in order to be respected. The people at Salvation Alley can touch me, they can feel me and Luke can vouch for me."

Through the passenger window, Julie observes a lady in her 60s, alone in her car on this beautiful Sunday morning. Alone in a world *teeming* with people.

Bart continues, "In TV-land they only go by what they see and hear. On TV, I can't be a King if I don't have a Queen."

Julie takes a deep breath. She looks at Bart with tears in her eyes.

"I'm just scared of what's gonna happen," she says.

Bart softly reassures her, "Julie, nothing's going to happen."

Julie nods her head and returns to the passenger window. Somewhere out there, beyond the traffic and the trees, her future exists. If she has a creator, Julie wonders, how cruel it is that she can't know her own fate. She wipes her eyes.

"Okay," Julie says.

"Okay what?"

"Okay I'll marry you."

Bart smiles to himself. He always knew the answer would be yes.

Julie, quickly recovered from her brief emotional lapse, points at Bart.

"But you better take care of me asshole!" she says half-jokingly.

Bart laughs, "I will, *Mrs Baxter.*"

Julie laughs an innocent laugh. Genuine.

With the marriage confirmed, Bart gives Julie a quick rundown of church etiquette. "Okay so today you're just going to sit in the front until I introduce you, then *I'll* come down to *you.* All you have to do is smile and grab my dick."

Julie looks at Bart in surprise and socks his arm. "I'll do it, don't tempt me Bart!"

Bart laughs through a grimace while rubbing his arm—Julie hits hard for a girl.

Still massaging his arm, Bart continues, "And you know the rules. No gum chewing, no kissing, no cursing. Just be a nice sweet angel to warm their hearts."

Julie looks at Bart disgustedly.

"Oh *fuck you* Bart."

Bart laughs at the unexpected comment, "Wait, what?!"

Julie punches his arm again. "Can I say that to you when you're up there on stage? Fuck you Bart! Fuck you? Huh? Will they like that? *Fuck fuck FUCK!*"

Bart pulls into the Salvation Alley parking lot laughing while Julie keeps cursing at him.

* * *

In the Pastor's office, Bart and Luke discuss business while Julie models her new church-friendly dress in the mirror.

"So before I introduce Julie today, I'm going to introduce our fundraiser for the new church."

Luke nods insecurely. He looks haggard sitting on the old gray couch, as if he hasn't slept well for a couple days.

"Alright. I put that goofy cross out there for you." Luke scratches his balding head, "You're sure about this?"

Bart nods confidently and begins to speak when Julie suddenly interrupts, "Fundraiser for a new church? I thought that lady gave you guys a million dollars?"

Luke looks at Bart with eyebrows raised; they've already had this conversation.

Bart explains, "Well Mrs Christianson gave *the church* a million dollars, but that's beside the point."

Julie's rarely privy to church discussions and frankly doesn't care what the boys do, but she likes to at least understand how it's all going down. She doesn't relent. "Okay, but you can still use it to buy a new church?"

Bart peeks over at Luke, who continues eyeing him disapprovingly, before offering an explanation to Julie.

"We need this congregation to donate for the new church so we get them locked into it before we go on TV."

Julie isn't following. She's starting to smell bullshit.

Bart continues, "It's equity Julie. If this congregation feels like they paid for the new church, they'll never leave it. I could piss on the altar and they'd still come back again next week. Plus, we'll have a nice, big congregation to show off for TV."

Oh it's bullshit alright. Julie knows it well, especially when it comes from Bart's mouth.

"It sounds to me like you just want to milk them as much as you can before they're dry," she says.

Luke acknowledges Julie with a nod and a grin as Bart submits with raised palms and shrugged shoulders.

Someone knocks on the door. Bart hollers, "Yeah come on in!"

The door opens and in walks one Bishop Ronny Patterson. Dressed to perfection in his white suit and hat, the man is *smoothness* personified.

Bart quickly rushes over to Bishop Ronny to welcome him and make introductions.

"Bishop Ronny, I'd like you to meet my brother Pastor Luke and my girlfriend"—Bart corrects himself—"um, fiancée, Julie."

Smiling, Bishop Ronny offers his hand to Luke who quickly coughs into his own hand and waves him off.

"Flu," Luke says through a feigned hoarse voice.

Bishop Ronny doesn't miss a beat as he turns to Julie and offers his hand. Julie shakes it and returns a warm smile.

Bishop Ronny turns back toward Bart, "And *you must be Pastor Bart…*"

Bart smiles and shakes his hand, "Pleasure to meet you Bishop Ronny."

Bishop Ronny narrows his eyes curiously at Bart and points at him from waist-level, "Have we met before?"

Bart confirms the meeting with a smile. "You came here about thirty years ago as a special guest of my father, Pastor James Baxter. I would have been a boy though."

Bishop Ronny stares narrow-eyed at Bart as he tries to remember the occasion. He looks over at Luke on the couch, then back to Bart. A sly smile slowly creeps across his face.

"You know I've been so many places over the years it's hard to remember just one." Bishop Ronny laughs under his breath while smiling.

Luke abruptly stands up, "Bart, I'm going out to the lobby to start welcoming people before the service." Looking at Julie, he offers, "Julie, if you join me I'll show you where you're sitting."

Sensing Luke's animosity toward Bishop Ronny and with no need to stick around the office, Julie agrees to go with him. The two of them pass by Bishop Ronny as they make their way to the doorway.

Julie sees right through Bishop Ronny's charismatic façade but is charmed nonetheless. She offers a wry goodbye, "Bye, *Bishop Ronny.*"

Politely yet still dripping with charm, Bishop Ronny bids her farewell, "Okay buh-bye now."

Luke and Julie disappear through the doorway.

Bart formally invites Bishop Ronny in and closes the door. He motions to the old couch, "Please Bishop Ronny, have a seat if you'd like."

Bishop Ronny walks smoothly toward the dusty old couch, takes a quick look at it, and decides to stand. He turns to Bart and poses a slowly spoken question to him, "So tell me Pastor Bart...*Why did you invite me here?*"

The question catches Bart off guard but he composes himself quickly. "Because I want to broadcast on your network."

Bishop Ronny laughs. He raises his eyebrows and mimics Bart, *"Because you want to broadcast on my network?"*

Bart's a bit intimidated by Bishop Ronny and feels a game of verbal tennis coming on.

"Yeah," comes Bart's flat response. A nice, slow volley back to the Bishop to see where this conversation is headed.

Bishop Ronny slowly tours the office, poking around at all the old, dusty items.

"And *why* do you want to broadcast on my network, Pastor Bart?"

Bart is at a loss for words as Bishop Ronny continues poking around.

"Hmm, Pastor Bart? No idea why you want to broadcast on my network?"

Bart steels himself. He looks directly at Bishop Ronny, verbal racket in hand, and smashes one right down the sideline.

"To make money."

Bishop Ronny looks at Bart and smiles. He stops poking around the office.

"Ah-hah! *To make money.*"

Bart holds his ground. It's *your serve,* Bishop Ronny.

"Can we talk real, Pastor Bart?"

Bart nods at the Bishop.

"I know you're a player, Pastor Bart, because every pastor on TV is a player. You want to be on TV because that's where the big money's at. And I don't blame you, because *I'm there too.*"

Bart listens as Bishop Ronny slowly circles the office again.

"But here's the thing, Pastor Bart. TV is *expensive.* You've got cameras to buy and you've got me to pay. TV is a beast that must be fed. So, Pastor Bart," Bishop Ronny looks at Bart, *"how are you gonna feed the beast?"*

Verbal tennis is about to end. Bart, finally informed of the game rules, is no longer intimidated by Bishop Ronny. He serves up what most assuredly will be an ace.

"Bishop Ronny, let me tell you about this preacher I saw on TV the other day who had a wonderful little story. The guy was a pastor's son who, for one reason or another, found himself in prison. The guards, they picked on this guy *every day* for reading his Bible. But sure enough, he made it out of prison *redeemed* by the blood of Christ."

A sly grin forms on Bishop Ronny's face as he listens to Bart.

"Born again, Bishop Ronny."

The Bishop's sly grin betrays genuine amusement.

"He took over the family church from his dying brother, then became so inspired by a dead widow's last request for a bigger church that *he started a fundraiser for it.*"

Bart steps toward Bishop Ronny as he speaks in a pleading tone, "Bishop Ronny, this guy could lay hands on people and *heal* them."

Bishop Ronny, eyes unflinching, wears a broad smile.

"Oh, and one other thing, Bishop Ronny..."

Bishop Ronny laughs softly through his smile as he raises an expectant eyebrow.

Bart's voice lowers, *"He could sing."*

Bishop Ronny chuckles to himself as Bart locks eyes with him.

The Bishop asks sarcastically, "He could lay hands on people and heal 'em?"

"Bishop Ronny," Bart looks at him matter-of-factly, "that's what I'm planning for my first televised show."

Bishop Ronny chuckles loudly in the quiet office. Seconds pass before Bishop Ronny winds down his chuckle, performed without ever breaking eye contact with Bart.

"That's good Pastor Bart, real good. I can see you're a man with a plan."

Bart gives a satisfied nod as the men break eye contact.

Bishop Ronny, still chuckling to himself, adjusts his suit prior to leaving. "Alrighty Pastor Bart, you let me know when you're ready to bring me a check. It's six-months' deposit upfront..."

Bishop Ronny looks at Bart knowingly, "I'm sure you can do the math on that?"

"Should only be a couple months or so," Bart replies confidently.

As Bishop Ronny heads for the door, Bart calls after him, "Are you staying to check out the service?"

Bishop Ronny turns in the doorway as Bart elaborates.

"We're starting a fundraising drive today for our new church," Bart adds sarcastically, "in case you want to donate."

Bishop Ronny chuckles again. "Nah Pastor Bart I don't need to see it, I'm sure you got it *well under control.*"

Walking out, Bishop Ronny mutters amusedly under his breath, *"This guy."*

* * *

Roughly thirty seats remain unfilled in the nave as we approach the two-minute warning before service begins. An ominous object, at least ten feet tall, stands on stage draped with red bedsheets. A nervous murmur fills the air as parishioners comment on the object. Julie sits in the front row next to the vacant seat sometimes occupied by

Bart. On the other side of the vacancy sits Luke; next to him sits a lifeless woman also known as Luke's wife, Diane.

A few older ladies whisper and point toward Julie. The words *Pastor Bart* and *very pretty* are read on their lips as they nod together. Elsewhere in the pews, teenagers and bachelorettes into their late-thirties sneer jealously.

The band is in place as Donny hums quietly to himself and nervously shuffles through his printed setlist. He checks his watch, looks up at the church clock, and adjusts his watch to synchronize the two.

Julie slowly drinks it all in. The band, the ominous object, parishioners glancing sideways at her. What a strange place to spend a Sunday morning.

Music suddenly begins playing. *Catchy* music. *Theme* music. *Bart's Theme Music.* The congregation takes to their feet and applauds as Pastor Bart Baxter walks out to the pulpit. Donny sings the words *hallelujah* and *glory to Him* as the music plays. Bart walks over to Donny and gives him a fist bump.

At stage-front, Bart looks to the ceiling and smiles as he raises his arms skyward. He points emphatically toward the heavens while repeating the words *Thank You Jesus.* Julie can't believe what she's seeing and has to bite her lip to keep from laughing.

Music and applause continues as Bart walks back to the pulpit.

"Hallelujah!" Bart yells into the microphone.

The congregation responds, "Hallelujah!"

Bart shakes his head and wags a finger at them. Over the music, Bart says, "Oh no, I'm not letting you off that easy!"

The congregation laughs.

Bart raises his voice to a yell, "*HAL-LE-LU-JAH!*"

"HALLELUJAH!" comes the roar from the congregation.

Bart sneaks a glance at Julie in the front row, still biting her lip. Her eyes are filled with love and pride for him. He raises a hand toward Donny and the band, still playing his theme. With one quick pump of the fist, Bart cuts the music.

* * *

Luke fights back a yawn as we reach forty minutes into the service. Bart stands on stage next to the ominous object, now uncovered and revealed to be a ten-foot-tall cross made of lumber with white vinyl attached to the face. Five horizontal marks have been drawn on the vinyl in equal intervals up the length of the cross. From the top down, dollar amounts are written in black at each interval:

$100k – $75k – $50k – $25k

The final mark at the bottom is simply the word *ZERO* written in all-caps.

Thick red streaks have been drawn over the *ZERO* as Bart stands to the side of the cross. In one hand, Bart fists an extremely thick dry-erase marker. The other hand holds the cap to the marker. Both hands are covered in red ink as Bart laughs with the congregation.

"Oh well I can wash it off. Or maybe I'll keep it there, after all it does represent *the blood of Jesus*." Bart raises a slick eyebrow and receives a few deep-throated *Amens* in return. Men always love hearing about the blood of Jesus.

Bart positions the cap back on the marker and pops it on. He walks behind the pulpit, places the marker on the shelf inside and inconspicuously wipes his hands with a towel.

"Now brothers and sisters, you know your Pastor likes to surprise you."

The congregation giggles nervously. They *do* like surprises.

Bart surveys them for a moment then speaks again. "Now we as Christians know that no man is perfect, *amen*?"

"Amen!" the congregation replies.

"And your Pastor is *certainly* not perfect."

A single *Amen* hails from the congregation.

Bart puts a hand over his brow and feigns looking for the amen rascal, "Who said that!?"

The congregation laughs.

Bart continues, "As Christians, we know that *only Christ* is perfect."

"Amen!" comes the unified reply.

"So Pastor Bart's gonna be honest with you and tell you that I've been, well…"

Bart pauses before divulging his secret to the congregation.

"I've been living in sin."

The congregation goes quiet as they allow Pastor Bart to speak from the heart.

"I've been engaged to the love of my life for oh, maybe ten years now. And well, I can't go back in time and stop sinnin', but I can certainly go forward and be a *better* man."

The congregation murmurs in excitement.

"A *Godlier* man," Bart says before looking directly at Julie. "A *truer* man."

The congregation eats it up; Julie eats it up too.

Bart returns his focus to the congregation. "Today is the day that I go forward as that better man. Brothers and sisters in Christ, I'd like to introduce you all to the future Mrs Bart Baxter—"

The congregation interrupts with a loud burst of applause. A few jealous hearts mix quiet sobs with their applause.

Bart shouts over the applause, "I hope you all will welcome her with open arms!"

Bart looks at Julie in the front pew. He begins walking down to her seat but she preempts him by rising up from her seat and walking up to him on stage. An instantaneous grimace flashes over Bart's face; he doesn't want Julie to make the wrong move. As she approaches him, he makes an awkward attempt to hug her but she quickly backs away. Not knowing what else to do, Julie shakes his hand and turns to face the congregation.

"Oh she's just being overly polite now, come on honey!" Bart tells the congregation.

The congregation laughs as handkerchiefs dab at moist eyeballs.

Julie steps backward and to the side of Bart. Now over her initial awkwardness, she implicitly knows the protocol for this moment. Sensing this, Bart decides to interact with her on stage.

In full view of the congregation, he looks back at her and speaks loudly off-mic so the congregation can overhear.

"Do you want to tell them or should I?"

Julie motions to Bart and responds girlishly, "You tell them!"

Bart smiles at Julie. He loves that she's playing her role so well.

He turns back to the congregation and asks in a low voice, "May I invite you all to the wedding?

The congregation, nearly frenzied by the wedding announcement, shouts as one, "YES!"

A few innocent catcalls ring out. Bart laughs and smiles.

"Okay well we're gonna have it at *this new church I've been hearing about...*"

The church explodes into laughter and applause as they babble hysterically in every direction. They speak to one other, they speak toward Pastor Bart and Julie onstage, and they speak to themselves.

Pastor Bart motions to a teary-eyed Donny and the band who quickly begin playing a jubilant Gospel song. Bart gives a smiling nod to the ushers in the rear, who begin hitting the rows with offering baskets. Then he waves Luke and his lifeless wife onto the stage.

Standing on stage from left-to-right are Julie and Bart, both smiling happily, and a haggard-looking Luke with his bewildered, lifeless wife. Bart's arms wrap around the shoulders of Julie and Luke, while Luke and Julie's arms wrap around Bart's waist. Luke's other hand clasps tightly to the hand of his lifeless wife.

* * *

Time lapses inside Salvation Alley church. As energetic gospel music plays, sixteen weeks go by one-by-one:

Julie sits smiling in the front pew, each week wearing a new church-friendly dress and hairstyle.

Pastor Bart preaches from the pulpit, each week sporting a new suit in a different shade of red. From the pulpit he mostly laughs, occasionally turns serious, and a few times pleads tearily with his congregation.

Throughout the time-lapse Donny wears his full suit in rich burgundy, singing boisterously with mic hand held high, medium or low. In a handful of instances, Bart appears with Donny and they sing together. Behind Donny, the band featuring Pops, Joey, Stoner Drummer and the Organist remains identical. Joey's scowl endures.

The fundraiser cross is slowly colored in by Pastor Bart as time progresses. Around the knee-high $10k mark, Pastor Bart hands the marker to Donny and invites him to color it. Donny struggles to bend down as Pastor Bart watches and laughs together with the congregation. Embarrassed, the big man eventually just takes a knee, adds some hasty red streaks to the cross, and reaches up uncomfortably toward Pastor Bart for assistance rising back to his feet.

Each week brings a linear increase in funds, except in one isolated instance featuring Pastor Bart wagging his marker angrily at the congregation and refusing to color. After sixteen weeks, the cross has been streaked red to the $75k mark.

Week-by-week, the congregation slowly grows. By week sixteen, every pew is filled. Salvation Alley has reached critical mass.

DRUNKS & PIMPS

Julie's breaking her own rule. As she drives down the freeway toward Bishop Ronny's Los Angeles office, Bart rides shotgun. He said he'd be using the phone a lot so she relented.

Bart dials the number he has for Bishop Ronny. Someone picks up.

"Hello, Bishop Ronny please? This is Pastor Bart Baxter."

Bart listens as the person on the other end speaks.

"It's in regards to a check I'm bringing him today."

Bart covers the phone and talks to Julie, "His secretary is putting me through." Bart snaps back to the phone, "Bishop Ronny, hey it's Bart Baxter. I wanted to bring that check to you today so we can—"

Bishop Ronny's tinny voice comes through the other end of the phone, loudly questioning Bart about something that Julie can't decipher. Bart looks very confused.

"Am I calling from a motorboat? No I'm in my car, why?"

A puzzled Julie looks over at Bart who's busy inspecting the passenger window.

"Yes, the windows are up—"

Bishop Ronny's questioning voice again comes through the phone, indecipherable except for the words *loud* and *windy*.

"No really I'm not in a boat," Bart flashes an incomprehensible look at Julie as he continues listening to the Bishop.

"No I'm not revving the engine." Bart decides to move the conversation forward, "Bishop Ronny look, I'm in my car and I'm coming to you today to drop off the check."

The tone of Bishop Ronny's tinny phone voice changes from questioning to curt as Bart listens. From Julie's end the conversation sounds completely ridiculous.

"Okay hold on." Bart covers the phone and turns to Julie, "He wants to know how old your car is."

The question annoys Julie. "Seven years, why?"

Bart uncovers the phone and responds, "It's seven years old."

Bart listens closely as Bishop Ronny gives him deliberate instructions.

Bart nods to the phone, "Okay. Alright."

Bishop Ronny continues before Bart interrupts him, "Alright well that might delay me a little bit bu—"

Bishop Ronny's tinny voice rises to a high, questioning pitch. Loud and clear through the earpiece comes the question, *"You sure you ain't in no boat?"*

"No Bishop Ronny I can assure you I am not driving a boat at the moment," Bart says while flashing a look of desperation at Julie.

"Okay. See you later today then. Yeah bye—"

The phone hangs up on Bishop Ronny's end. Julie looks over at Bart for the rundown.

"He said I can't bring a piece of shit car into his parking lot because it will, in his words, '*muddy up his image*'."

Julie rolls her eyes. "So what are you gonna do?" she asks.

Bart is matter-of-fact. He has no other choice.

"Looks like I'm gonna buy a car."

* * *

Julie drives down a familiar boulevard filled with auto dealerships. Known as the Cerritos Auto Square, it's billed as the World's Largest Auto Mall and features almost 30 domestic and import brands. Bart only needs one, but he's still undecided.

"Bishop Ronny said to get something nice and classy, nothing too flashy."

Julie continues driving as Bart looks around. They drive past a Cadillac dealership and Bart immediately lights up, "Bam! Cadillac!"

Julie ungracefully pulls her seven-year-old Nissan into the Cadillac dealership. Three bleary-eyed car salesmen stand in the shade near the front doors drinking coffee as they watch Julie pull in to the lot.

The eldest salesman, known by the other two as Chubbs, lets a question fly into the air in from of him, "You want this one Jimmy?"

Salesman Jimmy, sporting a well-groomed-but-sleazy lip moustache, also speaks to the air, "Nah you take it I'm busy."

Chubbs checks his watch. "I can't, I have a dump inbound in fifteen. What about you Freddy?"

Freddy, hair slicked back and eyes forward, replies, "Look at her car, Chubbs."

Julie, confused at the dealership's parking layout, unconsciously pumps her brakes as she tries to determine where to park. One brake light is out, the other winking intermittently as Julie circles the lot.

Slick Freddy speaks to the air, "She ain't buying shit."

The three salesmen sip their coffee.

* * *

Julie's still looking for the parking area when Bart tells her, "Just drop me off here, I'll get out."

Confused, Julie asks, "You just want me to drop you off and leave you stranded at the dealer?"

"I'll just drive the new car home," Bart replies confidently.

Julie stops the car but remains confused since she assumed Bart would need a co-signer to buy the car. As Bart exits the car, Julie hollers through the opened car door, "Bart! Don't you need my help to buy the car?"

Bart looks back and shakes his head at her with a grin. He flashes the church credit card he's carrying then closes the car door.

Through the closed window Bart yells, "Mrs Christianson wanted us to have a new car too!"

Julie flashes a disgusted look at Bart as he gives her the thumbs-up. Bart turns and walks away from the car as Julie shakes her head.

"What an asshole," she says to herself while pulling away.

Bart walks toward the salesmen, still drinking coffee as they idle in the shade.

* * *

From the shade, the three red-eyed salesmen watch as Bart exits the car and walks toward them. They quickly realize their prospects have improved.

Chubbs is first to act. "This guy is money, I'll get him."

Jimmy's moustached-lip quickly slurps the remaining coffee from his styrofoam cup. "I thought you had a dump in fifteen minutes," he asks.

"I'll hold it."

Slick Freddy also gulps down his coffee. He runs a hand over his slicked-back hair and pops a breath mint before staking his claim.

"Fuck you guys, I got him."

* * *

As Bart approaches the men, he observes them gearing up to pitch him. He mutters under his breath, "Alright you fucking sharks, *here I come.*"

Just as Bart reaches the men, fresh-faced rookie salesman Duong opens the dealership door. An extremely narrow Asian kid, Duong wears a tight white dress shirt tucked tightly into tight black slacks. His tie is too broad and too long, and his hair is too thick.

Duong hollers to Slick Freddy, "Freddy can you show me how to do a sales contract today?"

With fresh fish inbound, Slick Freddy quietly tries to hush the kid. "Not now you fucking mop handle."

Bart overhears Duong and instantly turns his attention to him as the other three offer hellos and handshakes.

"Young man, can you help me?" Bart asks.

Duong looks around before realizing that Bart is speaking to him. He replies nervously, "Ummm…Help you with what?"

Knowing he's being watched by the other three, Bart's eyes flash at young, fresh-faced Duong.

"Take me to the nicest car you have on the lot. *I'll be buying it today.*"

Duong nearly faints as the other salesmen deflate.

* * *

Out on the car lot, Duong and Bart are lost in a sea of sparkling new vehicles. As Duong escorts Bart through the lot making small talk, it's obvious to Bart that he's following a sales script.

"Ahh, what a nice day we're having," Duong says. He looks over at Bart, "So how has your day been sir?"

Bart comes close to rolling his eyes but holds back. He doesn't want to be rude to the kid.

"It's been fantastic," Bart takes a stab at the kid's name, "*Dong* is it?"

Duong is used to people not getting his name right and has given lessons on it at least once a week for the past fifteen years. He half-heartedly walks Bart through the pronunciation.

"Doo-ung."

Bart tries to repeat what he just heard, "Doo-Ong?"

Duong corrects him, "Doo-ung. You have to combine it together in the middle."

Try as he might, Bart's tongue just doesn't work that way. He gives up trying and just settles on what he can manage.

"Well Doo-wong my good man, I need to buy something classy today. Classy but not flashy."

Duong thinks hard. Where he lacks in self-confidence he makes up for with an incredible knowledge of Cadillac motor-vehicle inventory. He repeats the description to himself, "Classy but not flashy. Hmm okay…"

In deep thought, Duong scratches at his chin. He suddenly raises a finger—he knows exactly what will work.

Duong beckons Bart down the aisle, "Please follow me sir."

Duong walks down the aisle as Bart follows.

* * *

On the CT6 model line, Duong has the driver's side open as he invites Bart to enter.

"Please try this one on sir and see how it fits."

Bart slides into the leather driver's seat. He grabs the steering wheel, messes with the controls, and instantly likes the vehicle.

Duong makes a casual but scripted joke, "It looks good on you sir!"

Bart pauses to think.

He talks to the kid while exiting the vehicle, "Doo-wong I want you to sit inside, start it up, and tell me what you think."

Duong is confused. This scenario wasn't in his sales script.

Bart reassures him, "It's alright Doo-wong, get in there and start her up. I wanna see you in there so I'll know what I look like when I'm driving."

Duong bobbles his head then reluctantly agrees, "Umm, okay."

He slides in, grabs the wheel and looks at Bart. "Vroom," Duong says weakly.

Bart is growing exasperated with Duong's lack of confidence but he remains patient as he exhorts him, "No Doo-wong, *start it up* man!"

Duong immediately hits the push start. The vehicle rumbles to life and Duong laughs at Bart. Bart, in turn, laughs delightedly at Duong.

"Now rev the engine!" Bart urges.

Duong revs the engine. It growls. Duong growls.

Bart loves seeing Duong get in on the action. "How about the sound system? Turn it up so I can hear it!"

Duong needs no more encouragement. He turns the radio up as loud as it can go, then leans over in the seat and rocks his head to a hip-hop song playing on the radio. He one-hands the wheel and looks out the window at nothing in particular.

Bart gives Duong a few seconds to enjoy the good life before asking, "What are you imagining Doo-wong?"

Duong thinks to himself while getting his imaginary swerve on.

Through low eyes and a wide grin he replies, *"Bitches."*

* * *

Back in the shade of the dealership's roof, the three salesmen look toward the area where Duong took Bart. Duong's music is so loud it can be heard all the way to the dealership entrance.

"Dave ain't gonna like that," Jimmy says before slurping a fresh mouthful of coffee with his moustached-lip.

On cue, a highly irritated Sales Manager Dave exits the dealership and approaches the three salesmen. "What in the hell is going on over there?" he discreetly demands.

Slick Freddy replies, "Dong is going on over there, Dave."

Distant engine revving now accompanies the loud music. Sales Manager Dave can hardly contain himself.

"What the fuck guys, you're supposed to shadow him at all times!"

Slick Freddy offers an explanation, "Hey he insisted on going solo on this one. I tried to tell him."

"Oh Christ…"

Sales Manager Dave run-walks toward the music and revving as Slick Freddy laughs with the other salesmen.

"Looks like Ding-Dong the stickbug is going bye-bye."

* * *

Bart and Duong both laugh together as Sales Manager Dave comes running up behind them, tie flapping wildly over his shoulder. He sees Duong inside the vehicle and literally can't believe his eyes.

"Dung, what on *God's green earth* are you doing?!" Dave demands in a voice just below a yell.

Bart amusedly looks at Dave as Duong's eyes widen in fear.

Duong fumbles around trying to turn off the radio and the car while stammering out an explanation, "I—I was helping this gentlem —"

"Get out of the car Dung!" Dave is having none of it. He points at the ground where he wants the exiting Duong to stand.

As Duong stands on the mark, Dave eyes Bart with suspicion. He's lost his cool and forgets his manners as he questions Bart, "And who the hell are you!?"

Bart laughs sarcastically at Dave, who immediately becomes uncomfortable upon realizing that Bart is a customer.

"Who the hell are *you?*" Bart challenges.

Knowing he's made a grave mistake, Dave is now quite flustered. He pulls his tie down from his shoulder and lowers his tone, "I'm the manager here. And you are?" Dave offers his hand to Bart.

Bart puffs up. He wants to smack Dave's hand away but thinks better of it.

"I'm Pastor Bart Baxter…"

Dave cringes inside.

"And I'm buying *two* of these cars today."

* * *

Mitchell Alexander *does* shit. He *does* auto finance. He *does* summers with his wife at his Mexican timeshare, where he *does* margaritas made with ice from bottled water and then *does* his wife in the community jacuzzi. Today, he's *doing* a well-dressed guy named Bart Baxter. Dave briefed Mitchell on the situation. The situation is, in a word, *not good*.

In Mitchell's office, Bart and Duong sit allied on one side of the table as Mitchell gets the ball rolling. "So how has your day been Pastor Baxter?" Mitchell asks.

Bart has no more patience for these chump salesmen. "Well *Mitch*, it's gonna get a helluva lot better once I'm out of your office."

Duong looks nervously at Mitchell.

Mitchell, smiling, takes it right on the chin and asks for more. "Haha well I'll try and get you outta here as fast as I can Pastor Baxter!"

Bart rolls his eyes in contempt.

Sales Manager Dave walks in with a coffee for Bart. "Here you go Pastor Baxter! One coffee black, no sugar." His voice is just as phony as Mitchells.

Dave reaches for any kind of friendly banter he can find with Bart. "Sheesh no sugar no cream huh?"

Bart is completely disgusted with Dave at this point and isn't afraid to show it. "No *Dave*, we liked our coffee straight up in prison."

Bart stares at Sales Manager Dave, who looks to Mitchell for support. Mitchell's eyes are locked tight to the computer screen.

Dave makes a break for the exit, "Ahrrrkay, well I'll let you guys work on the paperwork and if you need anything just..."

Dave walks out and closes the door without finishing his sentence.

Bart turns to Duong, "Doo-wong would you like some coffee man?"

Duong makes a disgusted face and rubs his belly, "No sir it gives me the bubble-guts."

"Call me Bart, Doo-wong."

Duong smiles at Bart and nods.

After hearing about what happened on the lot and witnessing him in action firsthand, Mitchell prefers to limit his interaction with Bart Baxter. Unfortunately, some things require it.

Mitchell asks in a wavering voice, "Okay Pastor Baxter so just to clarify, you're buying two of these vehicles today correct?"

Bart stares Mitchell down.

"Yes." Bart lifts his fingers, "Two."

Bart looks over at a nervous Duong, "We got you the color you wanted, right Doo-wong?"

Duong's voice strengthens around his new pal, "Yep. Crystal White Tricoat."

Bart looks back at Mitchell, who can feel Bart's gaze scorching the side of his face. He *so needs* a Margarita right now.

Without looking away from his computer screen, Mitchell confirms the purchase. "Yes, I have here two CT6 sedans in the Crystal White Tricoat."

Bart looks at Duong and tells him quietly, "Great choice Doo-wong."

Duong smiles warmly, "Thanks Bart."

Mitchell's forced to interact again as he hesitantly begins selling Bart the extended warranty. "So Pastor Baxter as you know, even automobiles as well-built as ours can"—Bart's eyes are like lasers penetrating right through the margarita-filled core of Mitchell, who does his damndest not to wilt—"have issues that occur beyond the expiration of the standard manufacturer's warranty, and which can be quite costly—"

"Mitch." Bart's done with these hacks.

Mitchell stops talking and looks at Bart.

"No."

Mitchell is relieved. Dealership upsell requirements have forced him to keep poking at a bear that's tired of playing with him, but now through words and tone he submits to Bart.

"Okay let me just get this printed up so we can get you on your way."

Bart needs a break. He stretches, lets out a bored yawn, and stands up.

"Doo-wong, I'm gonna head to the bathroom for a few. Take care of the rest for me huh?" Bart tosses the church credit card on the table.

Duong accepts, "Yep, I got it Bart."

As Bart walks out he tells Duong, "I'll meet you at the cars in fifteen minutes."

Alone at the table, Duong stretches his arms with a bored yawn while Mitchell keeps his eyes on his work.

* * *

Bart wanders out of the finance office and looks for the bathrooms. Two janitors in their early 40s are busy cleaning a small spill in the lobby. One is short and runty, the other tall and overweight. Bart interrupts them to ask directions and immediately recognizes the two: Jerry and Larry, his bully duo from elementary school. If

Larry's beady little eyes weren't enough confirmation, Bart notices their names sewn into their work shirts.

Bart seethes inside but maintains his cool as he engages them. "Excuse me guys, where's the bathroom?"

Jerry and Larry point down the hall and speak in unison, "Over there."

"Thanks guys!" Bart replies.

Bart begins to walk away when he catches himself and returns to the duo.

"Hey do you guys have a compliment card box or something like that here? I'd like to drop a note in there praising you guys for your help."

Jerry and Larry smile together. Jerry has disturbing amounts of plaque on his teeth and Larry's beady eyes are made worse by his short, thin eyelashes. Again they speak and point together, "Over there."

"Hey thanks again guys!" Bart says with a fake smile.

Bart grabs a comment card and heads toward the restrooms while Jerry and Larry look at each other with excitement.

"We're getting a raise!" exclaims Jerry as he holds his palm up high. Larry jumps and high-fives it.

* * *

As Bart reaches the bathroom door, Salesman Chubbs walks out. Bart opens the door and is at once hit with a terrible smell. He looks disgustedly at Chubbs who walks flat-footedly down the hall, oblivious to the toilet paper hitching a ride on his shoe.

* * *

Outside, Bart's cars have just been pulled up to Duong at the vehicle release point. With a diamond cutter's eye for detail, Duong carefully inspects both vehicles per the dealer's presale checklist. He immediately sends both back for a wash.

* * *

Back in the lobby, Jerry and Larry man their mop bucket while staring through the dealership window at a happy young boy walking with his parents through the lot. Afflicted with a mobility issue, the child uses forearm crutches to aid in walking. As the smiling boy converses with his mom, Jerry begins quietly making fun of the child to Larry.

"Arr. Arr. ARR!" Jerry says as he manipulates the mop inside the bucket.

Larry hacks out an obnoxious laugh and grabs at the mop handle for his turn to make fun of the boy. Jerry's not finished yet and pulls the mop handle away from Larry too forcefully, causing the entire mop bucket to tip over. The small spill they were cleaning just increased in size by a factor of ten.

* * *

Comment card completed, Bart returns to the lobby as Jerry and Larry panic to contain their new spill. Water quickly spreads across the lobby floor as the two run frantically for orange cones. From his office, Sales Manager Dave sees them scrambling and shakes his head in disgust.

Bart, eyes steeled on his bullies, walks with card in hand toward the drop box. He gives it a quick review:

> *"Who do you want to recognize?* 'Jerry and Larry the asshole janitors.'
>
> *"What do you want to recognize them for?* 'My wife overheard them talking about her breasts in a very crude way.'
>
> *"Any other comments?* 'I will never set foot in this dealership again while Jerry and Larry are here to make sick comments about women's breasts.'"

Satisfied, Bart drops the card in the box.

* * *

Both cars have been freshly washed and inspected as Bart exits the showroom and approaches Duong.

"Well Doo-wong, it's one for you and one for me man."

Duong has tears in his eyes. This man Bart Baxter, unknown to him only a few hours ago, has changed his life. He's speechless as Bart gives him some stern ground rules.

"Now this thing is technically owned by my church but you're allowed to drive it, so don't go crashing the thing and don't sell it, alright?"

Dong listens closely and nods.

"And whether it's five months or five years, it comes back to me whenever you're done with it."

"Thank you Bart," Duong says emotionally.

"You're welcome Doo-wong. And don't take no shit from those other guys, they're chumps."

Duong laughs.

Bart gets in his new car and starts the engine. He turns once more to Duong, "And if you want to learn how to be a *real* salesman, come see me."

Bart turns the radio up full blast and rocks his head to a hip-hop song as Duong laughs at him. Bart closes the car door and drives off as Duong watches him leave, left to wonder why this mystery man would be so generous to him.

* * *

Forty-five minutes later, Bart's parking his car between two luxury sedans: a Lexus and an Infiniti. With the exception of a single red compact car, the few cars in this tiny lot are midrange luxury. Adjacent to the lot is a small round building resembling a miniature Great Western Forum. In front of the building stands a twenty-foot-tall cross with the letters *BFN* spelled down the center. Bart has arrived at the headquarters of Bishop Ronny's Blessed Flock Network. He exits his car and walks toward the front door.

Bart enters the lobby to find a muscular black security guard manning a desk with a phone and two closed-circuit monitors resting on top. Behind the desk are two closed doors. Above the doors, an electronic sign displays a bright red message: *Live Taping – Do Not Enter.*

The security guard is politely authoritative as he speaks to the visitor walking into his lobby. "Can I help you sir?"

"Yes I'm here to see Bishop Ronny." Bart approaches the guard desk but maintains a courteous distance.

"What's your name sir?"

"Pastor Bart Baxter."

The security guard picks up the phone and speaks to the other end, "I have a Pastor Bart Baxter here for Ron?"

Bart looks around to avoid staring at the guard. The floor and walls are carpeted in purple and gold and to his left is a hallway that winds around to the right.

The security guard hangs up the phone and briefly studies Bart up and down.

"You have any weapons on you?"

Bart is surprised by the question but quickly answers, "Uh weapons, no."

The security guard looks Bart over once more then points to the winding hallway on Bart's left.

"Alright, head down that way and I'll buzz you in."

Bart points himself down the hallway and begins walking. As he winds rightward along the curving hallway, Bart passes numerous life-sized color pictures of a young Bishop Ronny in various states of preaching, dancing, and singing. After a brief stroll, Bart makes it to a closed door with a surveillance camera mounted above it. As Bart approaches the door, it buzzes loudly. He pulls the door open and walks through it.

A very attractive secretary sits behind her desk, fifteen feet or so from the hallway door Bart's just entered from. To his left is a leather couch and two overstuffed leather chairs. Behind and to the right of the secretary is a closed door. The secretary wears a tight red top, a red sundress and red heels to match her red-painted fingernails. A nameplate identifies her as Grace.

"You must be the Pastor Baxter I've heard so much about," she says through a seductive smile.

Bart laughs uncomfortably—this is a dangerous woman.

"That I am. I'm here to see Bishop Ronny?"

Grace asks coyly, "And does Bishop Ronny know you're coming for him?"

Bart tries hard to stay professional as the secretary bats her eyes at him. He wonders to himself: *Is this some kind of weird test?*

"Well I uh, I spoke with him earlier today and let him know I was coming in, Grace."

Grace feigns surprise and places a hand on her chest.

"Pastor Baxter! How did you know my name was Grace?"

Bart is really being thrown off his game by this girl. He motions toward her desk.

"Well your name is right there on your desk."

With a hand still pressing against her tightly bloused chest, Grace slowly leans forward and grabs the nameplate. She looks at it, then delicately places it back in position.

Grace laughs softly, "Well if I'm Grace then who are you, *Pastor Baxter?*"

Bart has got to get himself out of this conversation. *What in the hell is going on here*?

He struggles with an answer to Grace's question, "Ummm…"

Grace playfully pounces on his indecisiveness, "Is it *Bobby?* Or *Billy?* Or—"

If ever there was a time for a man to pull the collar away from his neck and let steam fly out, it is now.

"Bart," he says plainly. "It's Bart."

Grace immediately softens as she gently blinks her eyes. She considers the name for a second then repeats it wispily to herself, *"Bart."*

She addresses Bart more formally, "That's a very nice name, Pastor Baxter."

Bart finally feels some relief. "Thank you Grace. That's a nice name too."

Grace blinks and smiles at Bart, then gets up and slowly walks to Bishop Ronny's door. She turns the heat up yet again as Bart is now forced to watch as she slowly sways to the door. She knocks once, then pushes the door open and leans in. From Bart's angle she appears to be teasingly bending over in front of him. As Grace closes the door and returns to her desk, Bart busies himself by looking everywhere in the room except at Grace.

"Pastor Baxter?"

Bart looks at Grace as if he just committed a crime.

Grace informs him matter-of-factly, "You can go in now."

Bart silently nods and walks quickly to Bishop Ronny's office door to make his exit from the steam room with Grace. He struggles as he tries to pull the door open; after fumbling with it for a few seconds, Bart realizes that the door actually opens inwards. Bart opens the door and steps inside as Grace laughs innocently.

* * *

Bishop Ronny sits behind a big wooden desk with two large monitors facing him from opposite corners. Behind him stands a well-stocked liquor cabinet. Mounted on the wall to his right is a bank of high-definition security monitors showing views from different cameras: the parking lot, lobby entrance, hallway door, Grace's office and other unknown locations within the compound are all under surveillance. On Bishop Ronny's left, a huge flat-panel display is mounted on the wall and tuned to BFN.

Bishop Ronny waits for the door to close behind Bart before saying, "So I see you've met Grace?"

Bart finally gets a chance to let off some steam and laugh. "Geez Bishop Ronny, what in the hell?"

Bishop Ronny laughs at Bart's reaction then waves it off, "She does that to everyone man but she's harmless."

Bishop Ronny motions to the parking lot camera, "So I see you got yourself a new ride?"

With Grace's full-court press still on his mind, Bart laughs again and looks at the monitor on the wall. "Yeah I picked it up an hour ago. Classy not flashy, right?"

Bishop Ronny chuckles, "Yes indeed, that certainly fits the bill.

He offers Bart some unsolicited style advice. "Now I ain't gonna tell you how to live your life Pastor Bart, but if it was me, I'd add a custom plate to that car. Something classy that people can get behind."

The thought never occurred to Bart but now that he's forced to think about it, he wonders to himself: *Can a vanity plate ever be classy?*

"Hmm. I'll consider that, Bishop Ronny."

Bishop Ronny hears the trepidation in Bart's voice. With a mentor's feigned deference toward his protégé, he replies freely, *"Consider it."*

Bishop Ronny moves on to business. "So what you got for me, Pastor Bart?"

Bart pulls out a check for $60,000 and places it on Bishop Ronny's desk.

"Six-months' deposit," Bart says confidently.

Bishop Ronny picks up the check and looks at it. With a sly smile he looks up at Bart, who makes one demand.

"We do the first show live."

Bishop Ronny's eyes narrow as he smiles at Bart's bold request. *"I can arrange that,"* he says, fingers smoothly caressing the check.

Bart nods, "Good." His own eyes narrow as he smiles back at Bishop Ronny.

"Now let's make some money."

Bishop Ronny laughs through his smile.

That's Entertainment!

The dust-caked Datsun is being towed.

Luke never felt the need to get rid of his dad's old car. After all, Salvation Alley under his watch was never at a loss for parking space. But tonight, with Pastor Bart Baxter's live television debut less than two hours away, Bart made the call. As the tow truck exits the lot with a tight right turn onto the thoroughfare, the Datsun it tows behind rolls off the curb. A cloud of dust poofs into the air as the vehicle vanishes into the oncoming night.

To the world, the church sign proudly trumpets:

Live TV Healing Tonight 7pm. All are welcome. Get Some!

At 5:30 p.m., only a handful of vehicles occupy the church parking lot. Included in that handful are Bart's Cadillac and a TV production truck, both parked up front near the church. The TV truck is busy extending its transmitter as an usher places a sign at the parking lot entrance:

Extra parking available across the street at Donut World

Across the street from the lot, an inconspicuous black van is parked under a street lamp. Joey exits from the driver's side, a cigarette burning red in his down-turned mouth. He walks to the rear of the van and opens the double door to reveal closed blackout curtains. Joey fishes around under the curtains until he hooks into something heavy. He pulls out his bass guitar case, closes the double door and takes a long drag off his cigarette while studying his reflection in the black-tinted rear windows.

Turning away from the van, Joey wears a smirk on top of his scowl. With a flick of his finger, he launches the still-burning cigarette into the gutter and begins walking toward the church, guitar case in hand.

* * *

Inside the church, television cameras are put through their paces as Luke converses with two big-boned gentlemen at the rear. Luke doesn't look well. On stage, Donny flits about nervously while Stoner Drummer adjusts his kit. The Organist tinkles the keys a few times but there's never much setup for her to do—she's always ready to rock.

Joey casually ascends the stage, bass guitar case in hand, as Donny approaches him.

"Hi Joey," Donny asks overpolitely, "did you talk to Pops?"

Joey scowls at Donny, replying in a low growl, "What about Pops, *Donny?*"

Stoner Drummer and the Organist watch from the sidelines as the conversation unfolds.

Donny responds with concern in his voice, "He called me earlier today and said he had car trouble and needed a ride. I told him maybe he could call you since you live out his way."

Joey shakes his head dismissively at Donny, "Nah I ain't heard nothin' from Pops today."

Donny's concern is growing but he maintains his polite demeanor: if there's one thing Donny hates, it's confrontation.

"Are you sure? He said he would call you right after we spoke."

Joey is becoming annoyed with the interrogation and growls out another response.

"Donny I told you I ain't heard from Pops today! *Got it?*"

Donny's face betrays the unsettlement he feels in his gut. He's genuinely concerned about Pops' well-being at this point but he's far too intimidated by Joey to press any further.

Joey leans in and takes a quiet sniff of the aroma wafting off Donny. *Fear.*

He looks Donny dead in the eye and tells him in a low voice, *"Ain't nobody gonna see Pops again."* Joey pulls back from Donny with a sinister smirk on his face.

Donny is frozen in place, face flushed and eyes wide in horror as Joey hikes through the band area toward his spot in the back next to the drummer.

Horrified by Joey's comments, Donny mutters under his breath, "Oh my *gosh.*"

As Joey reaches his spot in the back, Stoner Drummer laughs loudly in his direction and raises his hand ape-like over his head. He asks loudly, "Yo Joey what'd you do ta Pops man!?"

A faint smile creeps onto Joey's face as he puts his palm out at waist-level to receive some skin. Stoner Drummer slaps it with a satisfying percussive clap.

* * *

At the rear of the church, Luke's conversation with the two large gentlemen is winding to a close. The men, Big John and Rich, are the newly appointed church doormen. They both wear similar, poorly fit suits that catch and bunch on their inner thighs. The men might be brothers but Luke has never cared to ask and doesn't plan to anytime soon.

"So we just want you guys to make sure nobody is coming in here to stir up trouble for Bart. People hear TV and all-of-a-sudden everyone's a comedian."

The two doormen nod their understanding.

Luke continues, "And if there's anything really serious that needs my attention, just wave to me and I'll come down."

Luke musters a smile and some bullshit for the men to chew on, "Thanks guys, we appreciate the extra effort you're putting into the church. Pastor Bart would tell you himself but as you can imagine, he's really busy in his office preparing for tonight."

Together, the doormen smile at Luke.

* * *

Bart's office door is closed and locked. Inside, Pastor Bart Baxter is shirtless and sitting on the couch with Julie on his lap facing him. Bart is busy stupidly motorboating Julie's breasts through her shirt as she giggles at his dumb antics.

Julie's attention changes to Bart's body where numerous tattoos are visible. Dollar signs on both shoulders, a laughing clown face on his chest, the word *REBORN* in block letters across his heart—prison tattoos, none too large and as tasteful as prison tattoos can be. Julie grabs his motorboating head, raises it, and looks into his eyes.

"What would people think if they saw those?"

"What those?" Bart is still distracted by Julie's breasts and doesn't know what she's referring to.

Julie touches his tattoos, *"These."*

Bart looks at his tattoos and pauses as he thinks of an answer.

"They wouldn't care," he says.

Julie finds that hard to believe, "They wouldn't care?"

Bart shakes his head in dismissal, "Nope, wouldn't care."

Bart's simple answer leaves Julie puzzled.

"And how does that work? Aren't you supposed to be nice and clean"—Julie already realizes how mistaken she is—"and perfect for them?"

Bart looks at Julie and laughs. He gets up off the couch as Julie slides off his lap.

"I know you didn't grow up in church Julie so let me tell you," Bart pauses briefly to put on his shirt, "nobody in church cares about perfect."

Julie watches Bart as he moves to his wardrobe, searching for a tie.

"What they care about is *entertainment*. Fire-and-brimstone is meaningless unless it's being shouted at you by some lunatic screaming at the top of his lungs. Then it's *exciting.*"

Bart found the tie he wants. He puts it around his collar and begins to tie it.

"Sadness is boring unless tears are being shed."

Bart started too long with his tie. He unties it and starts over.

"Ask yourself this question Julie: 'Why don't people just stay at home and read the Bible all by themselves?'"

Julie ponders the question.

Bart preempts her thought with his own answer, "Because *it's boring,* Julie. The Bible is mind-numbingly, eye-crossingly, *dick-shrivelingly* boring."

Julie snickers at Bart's description. She enjoys listening to him.

"Church, on the other hand...church gives it *life.*" Bart raises a finger to emphasize, "A good church, that is."

Bart's finished adjusting his tie. He grabs a new pair of pants out of the wardrobe and begins changing out of the pants he's in.

"Sure, a boring church can stay afloat by getting a few lonely saps together every week to gossip and exchange business cards, but for a church to thrive?"

Bart tucks in his shirt and zips up his new pants—they're white.

"For a church to thrive, Julie, it needs to be *entertaining.* It needs music, it needs laughter, and most of all it needs a *leader* to look up to."

Bart grabs a white jacket to match his pants and slides into it. He continues his lecture while surveying himself in the mirror.

"It needs a shepherd who offers them reassurance every week. A person who tells them that in this great big scary world, *everything is gonna be alright.*"

Bart studies his face in the mirror. "That person isn't God, Julie." He dabs oil from his forehead with a towel.

"That person is me."

Bart turns away from the mirror and faces Julie. He lifts his arms out from his sides and, with eyebrows raised, awaits her assessment of his clothing choice.

From the couch, Julie gives him a double thumbs-up.

Bart approaches her and offers his hands. She takes them and looks up at him. Bart looks deep into her eyes.

"To these people, *I am God.*"

* * *

With forty-five minutes till showtime, two large padlocked boxes have been setup on opposite aisles of the church, near the rear seats and out of camera view. Signs affixed to the boxes read:

Healing Donations – Please give to the Lord

Like a giant thermometer, the Fundraiser Cross stands proudly in front of the band area, colored red to the $75k mark.

In front of the stage, a weary Luke is busy giving instructions to six suited ushers: Four originals, plus an additional two loyalists plucked from the congregation. All eager to serve the Lord tonight.

"Now understand that some people may fall backwards after being healed. We don't want them getting hurt, so we need to spot everyone and be prepared to catch them *before* they fall."

An usher named Bob, sporting a hideously thick beard that looks like it should be wearing underwear, raises his hand with a question. Luke nods to him.

"What if they fall *forward?*"

The wheels spin in Luke's tired head as he fights back the urge to just walk out of the building and away from this whole charade. However, duty calls and it *is* a valid point that he hadn't considered.

He drags his words as the answer comes to him, "Then…just…try and grab their shoulders to keep them from toppling forward."

Usher Bob is satisfied with the answer, as are the other nodding ushers who apparently had the same question.

Luke looks at Bob and thinks to himself: *Bob really needs to put underwear on that thing.*

Suddenly, a wide-eyed and deeply concerned Donny approaches Luke. Donny doesn't want to butt in but he has no other choice: *this is an emergency.*

"Pastor Luke I'm so sorry to interrupt—"

Luke is happy for the interruption. He'd much rather talk to Donny than the ushers. Donny is a good guy with a gentle, genuine kindness to him. The ushers are just stuffy old men trying to improve their seating assignments in heaven.

"Oh it's no problem Donny," Luke turns to Donny as he bids a final word to the ushers, "so remember, you guys watch Pastor Bart and follow his lead."

The ushers walk away as Donny explains his emergency to Luke.

"Pops didn't show up tonight."

"Pops…" Luke searches his memory, trying to place the name with a face. He hazily remembers, "The guit—"

"The guitarist, yes," Donny interrupts. It's unlike Donny to interrupt someone while they're speaking.

Luke quickly assesses Donny. This isn't the worst news in the world, it's barely even bad. But something has Donny terribly spooked and Luke needs to follow-up in order to settle the big man down.

"Is…he…*okay?*" Luke asks slowly.

Donny, wide-eyed, shakes his head. Luke isn't sure what that means.

"Did something *happen* to him?"

With Luke still studying him, Donny steals a glance over at the band. Joey, glaring intensely at Donny, shakes his head once. Ominously.

Luke's eyes don't move off Donny. The actual band requirements tonight will be very light but Donny himself might be called on for some announcements. Priority one is getting him stable enough to function.

Luke reassures him, "Look Donny I'm sure he's fine, he probably just had car trouble—"

Donny gulps air and sighs loudly. He looks like he's going to be sick as Luke tries to remember if the church has a first-aid kit.

Luke continues, "I'll let Pastor Bart know but don't worry, everything will be just fine. We don't need much music tonight so *I'm sure nobody will miss him.*"

Donny looks away and mutters under his breath, "That's probably what Joey thought."

Luke steps up and takes charge. "Look, get yourself outside and get some fresh air. Come on I'll walk you out."

Luke awkwardly pats Donny on his large, slumping shoulders, then puts a friendly hand on Donny's back and walks him to the front door.

* * *

Thirty minutes to showtime and the parking lot is packed full of cars. Across the street, cars spill over into the Donut World lot where business looks brisk.

Inside the church, the healing line is already taking shape on the left aisle. Ushers go down the line asking each person what they need healing for. Reported ailments are written on notepads.

"Fatigue," reports an elderly lady.

"Sadness," reports an elderly man.

A middle-aged man and his middle-aged wife are in the healing line together. From the looks of it, the couple is extremely conservative. A perfectly straight line, six inches in length, extends front-to-back across the man's scalp. It's a hair part whose strict precision could only truly be appreciated by scientists, generals, and dictators. The man's wife wears a monotone red dress that extends down beyond her ankles —without visible feet, she appears to float ghoul-like in the healing line.

The usher inquires of the couple, "What would you like healing for sir?"

With shifty eyes the man whispers breathlessly, "Sex addiction."

Behind the middle-aged couple, an old grandfather holds his granddaughter's tiny hand as he studies the stained-glass windows on the left wall. An usher on his right quietly asks what his ailment is, "Excuse me sir, what would you like healing for tonight?"

The grandfather ignores the question as he continues studying the stained glass.

The usher asks again, "Sir, could you please let me know what you need healing for?"

The young granddaughter looks up at the usher and yells loudly at him, *"He's deaf!"*

She yanks on her grandpa's hand; he looks at her as she points at the usher.

The grandfather turns to the usher and yells, "Huh!?"

The usher smiles politely while jotting on his notepad. Under his breath he spells to himself, "d-e-a-f".

The usher then moves down the aisle to the next person.

* * *

With twenty minutes to kickoff the ushers are huddled-up with Bart in his office, receiving instructions from their star quarterback.

Bart quickly reviews each man's notes and instructs, "Okay I want headaches in one group and I'll give you the word when to release them to me. Any guys whining about headaches get an aspirin on my mark. Wheelchairs and anything terminal gets parked in the front row where the cameras can see them."

Bart takes a pen and scribbles on one of the notepads. "One, two, three, four, five. Put 'em in that order. And keep your eyes on me boys, I might be calling audibles out there."

The ushers nod in unison.

Bart puts a hand in the huddle and looks at the ushers. They put their hands in, too.

"Okay, Jesus on three. One, two, three—"

"JESUS!"

* * *

Donny's back on stage with ten minutes to go, arms crossed while seated with his back squared to the band. The jovial, bouncy, pre-service Donny has been replaced with a silent, catty Donny. His lips are pursed tightly and his eyebrows are raised in extreme displeasure: Donny Davis is giving the band the cold shoulder.

The main healing line snakes down the left aisle toward the stage. The right aisle has its own healing line occupied almost entirely by women: those are the headaches. Ushers bring wheelchairs to the front row. A young mother with her baby is also brought to sit in the front.

Buried in the rear corner of the church is a table occupied by two laptops, two telephones, and two ladies: Mrs Evans and Julie. The table displays a large sign that reads:

Call now for healing! 888-LIV-HEAL

Julie is busy becoming acquainted with her laptop prior to the show. Seated next to her, Mrs Evans has her laptop firmly closed and pushed aside as she waits by the phone dutifully. Paper and pencils are in heavy supply.

A cleanly dressed but toothless homeless man wanders into the empty church lobby through the front doors. Big John, the lobby doorman, is missing. Just as the homeless man enters the church nave, Big John returns from the lobby bathroom and adjusts his crotch. With nobody around he farts, then suddenly freezes. His eyes drop low as he looks left and right, then dashes back to the bathroom.

In the nave, the homeless man joins the main healing line from the rear. The other doorman, Rich, is on the other aisle leering at the headaches. From his place on stage, Luke immediately spots the homeless man and hurries offstage toward him.

The homeless man flashes a polite, gummy smile at the people in line. Luke reaches him first with Rich converging quickly from the other aisle.

Luke addresses the homeless man in a friendly tone, "Hey Gary how're you doing tonight?"

Gary recognizes Pastor Luke; he's been giving him meals for years. "Is this the food line?" Gary asks.

Rich the doorman is now on-station. With an exasperated look, Luke motions discreetly to Rich and then to the front doors.

"No Gary this isn't the food line but Rich here will get you some food, okay?"

Gary doesn't argue; he simply raises a hand in thanks and nods politely at Rich.

Fresh from the bathroom, Big John hurriedly arrives to assist while pulling at the seat of his pants.

Irritated, Luke leans in and speaks softly to the doormen, "Can one of you guys please grab a snack bag out of the nursery fridge for Gary and *nicely* escort him outside?"

Luke gives both men a dirty look as they nod concurrence and begin walking up the aisle toward the lobby. Rich instructs Gary to follow him with a tongue click and a hand wave. Not knowing who to follow, Gary looks confusedly at Pastor Luke.

"It's alright Gary, go with them and they'll get you something to eat," Luke says reassuringly.

Big John decides to make things right with Pastor Luke by taking some initiative. "We got your food out here bud. Come on, let's go boy!" Big John pats his leg and whistles at Gary as Rich disappears to raid the nursery fridge.

Gary follows Big John into the lobby as Luke struggles to contain his anger.

* * *

With a minute before Pastor Bart's live television debut, a director sits in the production truck viewing a bank of monitors presenting different camera feeds. The stage is covered from multiple angles, including one showing the Fundraiser Cross and band area behind it. The call center with Julie and Mrs Evans has a dedicated camera, and two mobile cameras currently film the church sign and front row wheelchairs, respectively.

The jokester operating the Fundraiser Cross camera has zoomed tightly into the band area to capture Joey scowling as he fiddles with his amp.

In the truck, the director laughs at the monitor while communicating with his cameraman.

"Jesus get a load of that guy! He looks like a serial killer!"

The camera tilts down to Joey's hands—*smooth as silk.*

"Dude look at his hands, they're *hairless!* Wait wait, go up again!"

The camera tilts back up to Joey's face. This time, Joey is scowling directly into the camera. Startled, the cameraman quickly zooms out and pans away.

"Oh you big pussy!" the director teases.

A digital clock in the truck reads 6:59:50 p.m. The director gets serious.

"Okay we're live in ten!"

* * *

On one side of an old tube television sits a black-and-white portrait of a young couple. On the other side, a color photo of an elderly lady with her grandkids. Furnishings in the room are old and wooden, much like the lady who now sits on the couch with her walker close at hand. A grandfather clock dings away as the TV displays a message:

A Blessed Flock Network exclusive event...

The message fades out and is replaced by a series of new words, each slowly zooming to dissolve:

Live

Healing

God

Miracle

A new message appears:

Live Healing!

The word *Healing* dissolves, the exclamation point scrolls left, and a new message is created—a message of hope for elderly viewers:

Live!

That hopeful message slowly zooms to fill the screen.

* * *

A viewer sits on a chestnut-colored leather couch, six feet away from a massive seventy-inch wall-mounted television. Framing the TV are two vertically oriented paintings of a panther. The viewer's slippered-feet rest on a plastic-covered ottoman in front. From the right, a female hand wearing red nail polish delivers a glass of dark liquor.

On the television, *Live!* cuts roughly to a live image of the Salvation Alley church sign as Bart's theme music plays:

Live TV Healing Tonight 7pm. All are welcome. Get Some!

Donny's tenor voice comes through the television loud and clear: "Do *you* need healing?"

The front pews appear on-screen, full of wheelchairs and the young mother with her baby.

"Do *you* need prayer?"

The call center manned by Julie and Mrs Evans is shown, along with the sign on the table:

Call now for healing! 888-LIV-HEAL

* * *

Big John, still picking at the seat of his pants, looks disgustedly at Gary as they both wait in the lobby for Rich to return from the nursery. Applause is heard through the closed nave doors as Pastor Bart takes the stage. Rich finally returns, single-handing three small Ziploc bags and a tiny carton of apple juice. In his other hand he holds a baby carrot.

Pastor Bart's voice is heard through the doors, "Before we get started tonight, I want all of our church family watching at home and abroad—"

Rich snaps into the baby carrot as he holds the bags just out of reach from Gary.

"Okay Gary here you go," Rich says between crunches.

Pastor Bart's voice continues, "—to reach out to us here and help us while we heal these beautiful servants of the Lord..."

Rich holds the bags aloft as he walks toward the front door. Gary reaches for the food but Rich stays one step ahead of him.

"Come on Gary let's go boy." Rich ends his sentence with a beckoning whistle.

"So give us a call, won't you?" The congregation applauds as Bart finishes speaking.

Still chewing his baby carrot, Rich shoulders through the front door as Gary pursues him. Big John follows behind.

* * *

Outside the church, Rich dismissively announces each bag as he hands it to Gary.

"Cheese sandwich, goldfish, carrots"—Gary smiles as he recognizes each one—"and apple juice."

Rich finishes handing them over. Gary's eyes light up at the small carton of apple juice.

Rich and Big John stare disgustedly at Gary, hands now clutching small bags of toddler food. The bag of baby carrots looks a little thin.

With a small voice, Gary bids a slow farewell, "Thank you gentlemen."

The doormen just want him gone. Big John underhand waves Gary away from the church, "Yeah okay guy. Away you go."

Gary points to the men. In his small voice he has one more thing to say.

"And please tell Pastor Luke—"

Rich interrupts and begins to crowd him, "*Let's GO* come on! Shooh guy!"

Gary stays to finish his sentence, "Tell Pastor Luke thank you too."

Gary turns away from the men and begins walking. *Oohs* and *ahhs* ring inside the church as the doormen watch him walk down the street.

"That guy's pathetic," says Big John.

Rich replies, "He smells like poop."

From the corner of his eye, Big John glances guiltily at Rich.

* * *

On stage, Pastor Bart is addressing the conservative husband and wife tainted by sex addiction. Each of them is flanked by an usher, one on each side. The other two ushers man the base of the stage where the healing line ascends.

"These fine people right here are facing an addiction to smut and filth—an addiction to the Devil himself!"

Wearing a curious smile, Bart leans toward the couple and questions them both.

"Now, which one of you is it?"

The wife raises her hand as she casts shameful eyes downward.

Surprised, Bart smiles at her then looks at the husband and smiles at him.

"Really?"

The husband nods his head. With a look of tired desperation, he looks to Pastor Bart while filling his cheeks with air and blowing out. It appears the man's wife is fucking him to death.

Pastor Bart returns his attention to the wife. She cowers as he approaches closely.

"Sister?"

The wife is afraid to look up.

"Sister? Look at me."

She shakes her head and begins to sob. Pastor Bart gives a nod to the onstage ushers flanking her—*prepare for impact.*

Pastor Bart speaks powerfully, "Sister in Christ, the Lord commands you to look at me!"

The wife looks up at Pastor Bart, terrified and crying.

Pastor Bart yells directly in her face, "OUT OF HER, YOU DEVIL OF ADDICTION!"

The wife falls backward into the ushers' arms. She may have fainted.

Pastor Bart immediately looks over at her husband, staring wide-eyed at Pastor Bart. Bart's own eyes are wild, fiery, as he shoots a stern finger at the man and shouts, "OUT!"

The man falls backward into the ushers' arms.

The congregation erupts into praise as a camera moves in to capture both people on the ground, heads supported by ushers. The husband is smiling and stretching his limbs broadly. Apparently he just wanted a chance to lie down without his wife climbing on top of him. Next to him, his wife barks quietly to herself as the ushers drag them both away.

* * *

Gary walks toward a distant freeway underpass, happily humming Bart's theme as he trudges along the sidewalk carrying his bagged food.

A speeding car quickly slows next to him and a teenager shouts from the passenger window, "Hey look it's a fucking *bum!*"

The driver shouts across his passenger, "Uggh, he smells like a trashcan!"

Both voices laugh obnoxiously as the car speeds away. Unperturbed, Gary continues walking.

* * *

Back in the church, a pimply faced teenage boy stands on stage with Pastor Bart across from him.

Pastor Bart invokes his healing, "Be healed!"

The boy's eyes close and he immediately shuts down, but there's a problem—instead of falling backward, he's merely slumped his shoulders and deadened his arms heavily like a sleepwalking zombie. His head hangs off to the side and there's a very real risk that he'll begin drooling soon.

Bart glances at the ushers who return blank looks. The kid has malfunctioned and his legs are getting wobbly. He pitches forward slightly as the ushers grab his slumped shoulders to steady him.

Pastor Bart calmly places a hand on the boy's forehead. In one smooth movement, Bart steps forward while driving the boy's head backward and speaking gently, "DOWN-down-down-down-*DOWWWN!*"

The boy lands comfortably in the ushers' arms.

Pastor Bart turns to the congregation with one hand pointing to the sky, "The good Lord's not making it easy on me tonight, brothers and sisters!"

The congregation laughs and applauds.

Pastor Bart is working himself up as he paces across the stage. Beads of sweat form on his forehead. He beckons loudly to the front row where wheelchairs and the young mother with baby sit.

"Do you want healing!?" Pastor Bart reaches his hands toward them.

They reach back and shout, "Yes!"

Bart calls to the front row again, "Tell me, what do you want!?"

Still reaching for him, the front row plus a few others in the congregation shout back, "Healing!"

Pastor Bart places a hand to his ear, *"God can't hear you!"*

The entire church shouts, "HEALING!"

Pastor Bart crows to the sky, "WHOOO!"

* * *

On the old lady's tube television, Pastor Bart screams out to the sky as her grandfather clock dings once. She points a remote control at the television and holds down the volume button. It begins counting up from 70.

Pastor Bart walks to the end of the stage where one of the mobile cameramen stands filming. He looks into the camera and quietly tells viewers, *"Watch this."*

The television volume hits 100.

* * *

Pastor Bart is a man possessed. His nostrils flare and he sweats profusely as arteries bulge in his head and neck. A man wincing in pain is gingerly helped on stage by the ushers as Pastor Bart addresses the congregation.

"Now, this man here has a frozen back that needs fixin'. Hell, we've all been there. You're pulling the weeds and suddenly you throw a rod and get that evil tickle in your backbone. Next thing you know, you're laid up on the couch all day like a *suckass* watching Jerry Springer on the TV!"

Many parishioners cover their mouths and laugh at Pastor Bart. Others pooh-pooh him innocently and dismiss him with a friendly gesture. Mild profanity by their Pastor is acceptable in service to the Lord.

Pastor Bart mutters an aside, "Hey I don't turn him on, he just shows up on the TV somehow."

More innocent laughter from the congregation as Pastor Bart cops to watching Jerry Springer.

As the back-pain man winces on stage, Pastor Bart's tone turns serious again.

"Now, I *needn't remind you all* that our God is a powerful God! I *needn't remind you* that he killed seventy men for merely *looking* into the Ark!"

Pausing, Bart looks sternly at his congregation. *Amens* are hurled at him.

"I *needn't remind you* that God turned Lot's wife into *salt!*"

More *Amens* come in as Bart's intensity grows.

"SALT!" Bart shouts. His voice echoes off the church walls.

"I sometimes wonder if the abundance of salt on this earth is evidence of God's almighty wrath," Bart raises his voice to a yell, "FOR WOE IS HE WHO DOUBTS THE POWER OF GOD!"

A final round of *Amens* rain on Pastor Bart as he stands firm, staring intensely at his congregation.

A low murmur radiates from the congregation. Agreement. *Anticipation.* Something masterfully divine is coming from their Pastor, and they'll be here to witness it.

Pastor Bart suddenly turns to the man with back pain. The man is flanked on each side by an usher, with two more standing behind him. Pastor Bart angrily removes his jacket and throws it to the floor behind him. The back-pain man now knows he made a terrible mistake coming here; he should have just stayed at home with a muscle relaxer and Jerry Springer. He looks around despairingly for an exit, but he's blocked in on three sides by ushers. The fourth side, his front, is blocked by a soon-to-be-rampaging bull named Pastor Bart Baxter.

Pastor Bart, nostrils flaring, glares at the man. If Bart had hooves he'd be using them right now to tear at the stage surface.

With a menacing grin, Pastor Bart approaches close to the back-pain man. In a calm voice dripping with sarcasm, Bart asks, "Do you know that God is here tonight?"

Bart points to the ground. "Right here, in this place."

Petrified, the man nods and nervously diverts his eyes from Pastor Bart.

With an uptick in his voice, Bart inquires wryly of the man, "Are ya *scared?*"

The man combines a nod with a shake, producing a head which moves diagonally—he's not sure which answer to give.

Bart mimics the man's diagonal head movement and asks dryly, "Is that a yes?"

This time the man nods his head. *Yes, he's scared.*

Bart gently puts his arms on the man's shoulders and leans toward him. He whispers in the man's ear, "Good. *You should be."*

Pastor Bart suddenly grabs the man in a violent bear hug and lifts him up off his feet. The man cries out like a wounded animal while ushers keep his arms pinned to his sides.

A wild-eyed Bart smiles madly as he shakes the screaming man up and down. The man, held tightly to Pastor Bart, grunts and screams horrendously as mortal fear clouds his eyes.

Pastor Bart yells at the man as he shakes him, "Cry out to God!"

The man is muted by pain.

Pastor Bart continues shaking him up and down as he yells again, "Cry out to God! He can't heal your pain until you ask Him!"

The man grunts and wails, *"God please help me!"*

Pastor Bart releases the man and lets him fall into the arms of the ushers.

The ushers bring him down to the floor as he moans in pain, tears streaming down his cheeks.

In delirium, the man moans softly, "Ohhh…thank you God… thank you God…ohhh…"

The congregation is on pins and needles. Pastor Bart looks down at the man and raises his hand to keep the congregation hushed.

"Do you hear that? Can you hear this man?"

Pastor Bart grabs a microphone, crouches down and puts it to the man's mouth.

Eyes closed and streaming tears, the man is nearly passed out from shock and pain as he whimpers, "Thank you God…ohhh thank you God…ohhh…"

Pastor Bart rises and turns to the congregation as he proclaims loudly into the mic, "He says thank you God!"

Bart lowers his mic to waist level, pausing to accept wild cheers from the awestruck congregation.

He looks back down at the man then raises the mic up to his grinning mouth.

"God says you're welcome!"

Thunderous applause fills the church as the congregation nearly loses control of itself.

The moaning man is dragged off by the ushers to reveal the next person in line for healing—a wide-eyed little girl holding a torn teddy bear. With terror-filled eyes, she looks at Pastor Bart and blinks.

* * *

Julie and Mrs Evans are being broadcast live from the call center camera. The sound of Pastor Bart speaking softly to the little girl is drowned out by ringing phones. Julie and Mrs Evans click between phone lines as fast as they can but they're becoming overwhelmed.

For viewers, a graphic overlay appears at the bottom of the screen:

CALL NOW FOR HEALING! 888-LIV-HEAL

Below the graphic a crawl is displayed to let viewers know their healing requests are being recorded:

Mrs Nancy-Swollen Feet – John in Saddleranch, KY-Piles – D. Hard-Priapism

The broadcast cuts from the call center to the Fundraising Cross. Phones continue ringing loudly over Bart's conversation with the little girl. A new graphic overlay replaces the previous one:

OUR CHURCH IS OUT OF ROOM! WILL YOU HELP US GROW? 888-LIV-HEAL

A donation crawl appends the healing crawl:

Randy $10 – Barb $100 – Ray $20

* * *

Back in real-time, Pastor Bart is stooped down and speaking gently to the little girl as a camera maneuvers in close to her.

"Can you say *please Jesus buy us a new church?*"

Pastor Bart places the mic to her mouth but with the camera so close, the girl is bashful. Bart coaches her along, mouthing the words for her to follow.

The girl speaks hesitantly, "Please Jesus…buy us a…new church."

The congregation fawns and claps for the little girl as Pastor Bart mugs for the camera.

"*Oh so precious…*"

The girl beams and hops at the positive attention. She motions to Pastor Bart for the mic back. He leans down again and mics her.

"And, um…please Jesus *buy me a new teddy bear!*"

The congregation laughs as the little girl laughs too. Bart mugs for the camera again.

Pastor Bart raises the mic to his mouth and looks at his ushers. "Can we please buy this little girl a new teddy bear?" he pleads.

The ushers nod and give him a thumbs-up, but the question wasn't meant for them. It was meant for the television audience.

Bart pretends to quarrel, "No no, I don't care if we can't afford it! Take it out of our emergency funds!"

The congregation applauds Pastor Bart as the little girl is lead away.

An attractive middle-aged woman is brought forward to Pastor Bart, squinting in slight discomfort. Bart places a finger to his lips as he looks at the lady. Not a word is spoken as he studies her intently.

Bart lifts his head to the sky with hands clasped together in mock prayer. The congregation watches as Pastor Bart prays to the heavens.

Bart nods dramatically to the sky, looks at the congregation and again places a finger to his lips. The congregation hushes. Pastor Bart approaches the lady and speaks to her softly.

"And how long have you had this headache?"

The congregation *oohs* at Pastor Bart's apparent divining of the lady's pain complaint. They don't know that he's hand-picked everyone being brought to him for healing. Even if they knew, *they wouldn't care.*

The woman responds softly to Pastor Bart, "Since this morning."

Bart continues in a soft tone, "Well tonight, by the power of God, your headache goes away. *Would you like that?*"

"*Yes.*"

The interaction between the two of them is becoming a little creepy.

"All you have to do is ask. *Tell God what you want.*"

The woman tells God what she wants. "Please God, *heal my headache.*"

Bart gently places a fist on top of the woman's head. With his other hand, he hits the fist with an open palm. A cracking noise echoes across the stage as Bart slowly draws his fingers down her head with both hands. It's the egg game—*Bart's playing the egg game.*

The woman shudders in delight as imaginary yolk runs down her scalp. "It's so warm and soothing," she moans.

The creepiness continues from Bart's end, "That's *God's love* ridding you of your headache."

Bart steps away from the lady, still basking in the warmth of an imaginary egg that's been freshly cracked on her head. He calls out with authority, "Ushers, empty the lines! I want all headaches around me *now!*"

The ushers quickly assemble the female headaches around Pastor Bart. The first woman, eyes closed and smiling, remains in place near him.

Pastor Bart, laser focused, immediately begins cracking imaginary eggs on real heads. As eggs are cracked, women *ooh* and *ahh*. The few men with headaches are corralled on the side of the stage, far away from Pastor Bart. Ushers ask the men to stick their tongues out for healing. An aspirin is placed on each tongue and a paper cup of water administered. One man stares enviously at the women receiving egg cracks.

Pastor Bart cracks his last egg and is now surrounded by cooing women. He whispers to a nearby usher, "Give each one an aspirin and get 'em seated comfortably in the rear."

* * *

The freeway underpass is fenced in by old chain-link; litter and garbage are strewn at its base. With the backlit cross of Salvation Alley in the distance behind him, Gary approaches the fence. He lowers himself to the ground and crawls under the fence on his belly to reach the other side.

* * *

The healing service continues with Pastor Bart. Another teenage boy has made it on stage and now stands across from him.

"And what has the devil done to you, son?"

The boy replies, "He ma-ma-makes me stut-tut-tutter."

Pastor Bart raises a scornful eyebrow at the boy. "He makes you stut-tut-tutter?"

The teenager nods his head, "Mm-hmm."

Bart walks away from the boy, shaking out his hands and arms. He reaches the far end of the stage and turns back toward the boy. Nostrils flare again as Pastor Bart looks directly into a mobile camera, "I need your prayers at home!"

Pastor Bart looks to the congregation. "I need your prayers here, now! Lift your voices to Him!"

The worshippers raise their voices in praise and prayer. Hands reach out to Pastor Bart.

Pastor Bart turns back to the camera and points at it.

"I can't hear you at home! Pray! NOW!" Bart commands.

The teenager looks bewildered and terrified—*is he about to become a human sacrifice?*

Bart shakes his hands and arms once more as the congregation buzzes loudly with prayer. He stomps back to the boy while shouting, "I strike out you devil of speech with the hand of God!" then slaps the boy.

The congregation immediately silences while continuing to reach their hands to Pastor Bart. Many of them have tears in their eyes.

"Speak boy! Speak!"

The teenager, shocked at the strike and with eyes full of tears, is speechless.

Bart approaches closer and growls, *"I said speak boy!"*

The boy can't find the words.

Pastor Bart leans in menacingly and roars, "NOW!"

The teenage boy explodes in a screech, "JESUS!"

The congregation erupts.

* * *

As distant shouts and music echo from far down the road, Gary reaches his unlit den under the freeway. He sits down and finally gets his chance to remove the sandwich, carrots and goldfish from their bags.

Gary calls out to the surrounding darkness, "Hey George I've got some dinner."

In the dark of the underpass, a friendly dog emerges.

Gary digs in the dark and finds a dirty bowl. He dumps the sandwich, carrots and goldfish into the bowl as his friend George approaches him.

"There you go bud that's good for ya!"

Gary pets the dog behind the ears as George eats from the bowl. He leans back, opens the apple juice and drinks it for himself.

The backlit cross of Salvation Alley shines in the distance.

* * *

The closed mini blinds of Pastor Bart's office glow in the light of a full moon. Hours after his television debut, he and Julie are the only souls remaining at Salvation Alley. Bundles of cash are rubber-banded and stacked by denomination on a large table that's been setup in the office. Pastor Bart's Bible also rests on the table, askew and to the side of the cash bundles. Bart lies exhausted on the old couch as Julie sits at the table, reading from a small stack of papers as she inputs numbers into a calculator. Her eyes are wide in disbelief.

"Bart, *do you know how much money you made tonight?!*"

Bart is exhausted. He replies wearily, "A million?"

Julie doesn't laugh. She's very serious.

"Close."

She looks at Bart as he lies on the couch.

"Almost *thirty thousand dollars*, Bart."

Bart laughs as Julie looks back at her stack of papers.

"Three thousand came in through the doors, the rest came through the phones and internet."

Bart laughs again. He's not surprised, but the amount of money is unbelievable to Julie and she wants his attention.

"Bart, a thousand bucks in phone donations was *specifically marked* to buy that little girl a teddy bear!"

Julie stands up and walks over to Bart as he lazily sits up on the couch. She looks worried.

"Bart…*what are you doing to these people?*"

Bart looks up at Julie and smiles.

"I'm *entertaining* them, Julie."

Julie sighs. She understands him, but the reality of the situation is still overwhelming.

Bart's eyes turn sharp, wolf-like, as he looks at Julie. He stands up and slowly walks her back to the table, Julie locking his gaze and retreating fearlessly.

At the table, Bart reaches around her and grabs at the bundles of cash. One-by-one, Bart breaks the rubber bands and rains bills onto the table as Julie watches. Bart lifts Julie up and seats her on the cash-covered table. Smiling, Julie lies back on the cash-strewn table as Bart begins kissing her.

Next to them, covered in bills, is Bart's Bible.

UNCHARTED TERRITORY

In Bishop Ronny's parking lot, a familiar mob of midrange luxury vehicles is assembled along with their decidedly *nonluxury* compact red friend. A Cadillac pulls into the lot and fits right in.

At his desk in the lobby, the muscular security guard is talking on the phone as Bart enters. Behind the guard, the *Live Taping – Do Not Enter* sign glows red as muted organ music accompanies a man's voice on the other side of the studio doors. Bart approaches the guard desk.

The security guard speaks into the phone, "Hey yo Ron, your *boy* is here."

Bart looks at the guard and realizes he's being discussed.

The guard looks at Bart as he replies to the phone, "Alright."

The security guard hangs up the phone and stands up. He motions to Bart to spread his arms out to his sides. Bart is surprised but complies. The guard frisks him quickly.

"Alright Pastor Baxter you remember how to get there?"

The muscular guard stares at him. Bart's feeling a negative vibe from the man but has no idea why.

Bart replies politely, "Yes, just down the hall here."

The security guard looks at Bart and nods. *"Right,"* he says flatly.

Bart wants to break this unnecessary formality between him and the guard. "Hey feel free to call me Bart," he offers.

Standing firm in front of Bart like a chiseled onyx statue, the security guard just stares at him.

"Right down the hall there, Pastor Baxter. Pull on the door when you hear the buzz."

Bart avoids pressing further with the guard. "Okay thanks," he says as he begins walking down the hall.

As Bart walks down the hall, his eyebrows furrow in confusion as he wonders why the guard has suddenly become unfriendly to him.

*　*　*

Bishop Ronny's secretary Grace, again wearing a tight red blouse, sundress and heels, is on her hands and knees in front of her desk searching for something. With her rear toward the hallway door, the sundress is dangerously close to exposing her sun, her moon, and everything in between to anyone entering from the hallway door.

The door buzzes and Bart enters. Grace doesn't flinch an inch. Bart immediately sees her on all fours and rolls his eyes within his rolling head. The only way to Bishop Ronny is through Grace so he has no choice but to approach her, but he's tired of her antics.

As he approaches, she sways left and right as she continues fishing for what Bart believes is absolutely nothing under her desk.

Through gritted teeth Bart speaks hesitantly, "Hi Grace."

Grace feigns surprise as she looks up at Bart.

"Oh hi Pastor Baxter!"

Bart smiles sarcastically at Grace.

She reaches toward him while struggling to get to her feet. Bart, being the only other person in the room, offers a hand to help her up. Grace grabs it and rises uncomfortably close to Bart—*did her thumb just caress his hand or is he imagining things?*

Still latched on to Bart's hand, Grace looks into his eyes. "Thanks Bart," she says softly.

Bart doesn't want to be impolite but this girl just keeps pushing him.

"You're welcome Grace," Bart says flatly.

Grace gives Bart a pouty look and releases his hand. She walks back behind her desk and turns to Bart.

"I'm not afraid of the *big bad wolf,*" she says seductively.

Bart's eyes glaze over and nearly cross in temptation. If he were a cartoon, his tongue would unroll from his mouth while steam shoots from his ears.

Bishop Ronny's office door mercifully opens and out steps the man himself, smiling broadly with his arms held out at his sides in a welcoming gesture.

"Pastor Bart Baxter the *miracle man!*" Bishop Ronny shouts.

Ronny laughs as Bart, still fuzzy from Grace's advance, looks at him. Grace claps and laughs at Ronny's enthusiastic welcome for Bart.

The Bishop beckons Bart into his office, "Come on in man!"

* * *

Ronny enters his office, followed closely by Bart. The Bishop motions to the door and Bart closes it.

Bart is still distracted by Grace's antics as Bishop Ronny walks to the liquor cabinet behind his desk to pour a drink.

"You want a drink, Pastor Bart?"

Bart replies without thinking, "Yeah and I'm gonna go pour it over Grace's head."

Bishop Ronny laughs at the spontaneous outburst, but Bart looks very annoyed. Recognizing Bart's irritation, Ronny addresses the issue.

"Okay okay, she's harmless man but I'll tell her to cool it when you're around."

"Yeah, *harmless,*" Bart says under his breath.

Ronny laughs again then changes the subject with an ice-breaker he likely knows the answer to.

"So did you get that big thermometer colored up yet?"

Bart puts the Grace shenanigans out of his mind and returns to the present.

"Oh yeah, *that* thing…" Bart returns to his normal self as he elaborates, "Bishop Ronny, I'm happy to report that our Fundraising Cross is now painted completely red with the blood of Jesus—"

Ronny gives a sly laugh.

"—and we'll be moving in to our new church at the end of the month."

Ronny smiles, "That's good, Pastor Bart, because I think *you're gonna need the extra space.*"

Bart nods in agreement as Bishop Ronny laughs through his smile.

Ronny pulls some papers out of his desk drawer and places them on the desk, facing Bart.

Bart looks at the papers lying on the desk. They're filled with graphs and numbers which make little sense to him.

"What's this?" Bart asks.

"That's *you*, Pastor Bart."

Bart looks confusedly at Bishop Ronny.

Ronny explains, "Those are your TV ratings, *Pastor.* You see that chart right there, that *big green bar?*"

Bart looks and nods.

"That's you."

With a pen, Ronny points at the other much smaller red bars on the graph.

"And these little small ones here? *That's everyone else.*"

Bart looks up at Bishop Ronny with his eyebrows raised in surprise. He laughs as Ronny smiles.

"Now I'm not gonna ask how much you've been pulling in, but I want to give you a suggestion moving forward…"

Bart listens attentively.

"Get yourself setup in that new church, get a few shows in the loop for the network, then go take a trip with that girl of yours and relax."

Bart reminds Ronny, "Actually, we're getting married at the new church."

Bishop Ronny listens as Bart continues.

"That was the deal for the congregation, we get married in the new church. I can't take a trip before that."

Bishop Ronny nods his understanding. "Good, so then you two have a reason to go on a honeymoon *of sorts.*"

"Right." Bart and Ronny are on the same page.

Bishop Ronny pulls out a resort brochure from his drawer and displays it to Bart.

"Now this here's a place where *a lot of us* go."

Ronny dons a pair of reading glasses as he opens the brochure. Pen in hand, Bishop Ronny points at the pages like a travel agent. Even the tone of his voice brightens as he reads the resort description verbatim from the brochure.

"The Resort *Fan-tas-tique*. Take a stroll in your own private garden as you bask in the calm elegance befitting one of the most prestigious hotels in all of Monte *Carlos,* France. With sunshine as your guide, navigate among"—Ronny corrects himself—"among*st*...the many luxurious pools…"

Bishop Ronny peeks at Bart as Bart eyes the other side of the brochure. Ronny hands it over.

"You keep that one. Go there with your girl and nobody's gonna bother you…"

Bart looks over the brochure.

"The last thing you need right now, Pastor Baxter, is some *paparotzee* snapping photos of you and Mrs Baxter gettin' busy on a beach somewhere. You got-to-be-discreet now my brother, you're entering the *high rollers club* and lots of people are gonna be looking out for you if you catch my drift."

Ronny pauses to make sure Bart understands.

"Ya feel me?"

Distracted by the brochure, Bart looks up at Bishop Ronny and nods.

"Yeah I hear you."

"Now, there's one more paper I didn't show you—"

Ronny pulls an additional piece of paper from the drawer and places it on his desk. Bart immediately places the brochure to the side and looks at this new paper.

"This one shows your ratings out in the *Orient,* country by country."

Bart looks over the paper as Bishop Ronny again uses his pen to point at the chart.

"You see this long green bar right here?"

Bart eyes the green bar then looks at Bishop Ronny and nods. The Bishop laughs to himself. Different than other laughs, this one is a laugh of disbelief.

"We'll go ahead and call that one *off the charts.*"

Bart and Bishop Ronny exchange perceptive looks. Bart speaks first.

"So you're saying I'm big in Japan*?*"

"Off-the-charts."

Bart wants to hear the Bishop's advice. "So what do you suggest, Bishop Ronny?"

Through his smile, Ronny laughs at his young protégé. "After you get your fill of France, buy yourself a ticket to Japan."

With eyebrows raised and a smirk on his face, Bishop Ronny looks Bart dead in the eye.

"Nigga you goin' on a *crusade.*"

Synchronicity

The parking lot of the new church is much larger than the old church, and by 9:30 a.m. half of the spaces are already occupied for opening day. More cars pull in as excited parishioners wave, smile and meet with each other before heading on toward the main church building. With a brilliant sun shining down on it, the church sign proclaims:

Jesus is here! Join us on TV!

Directly outside the main church entrance a banner reads:

Pastors Bart and Luke Baxter welcome you to your new home!

Manning the doors are big-boned doormen Big John and Rich, wearing their Sunday-best rack suits, pants still grabbing at their thighs.

* * *

An electronically tinted second-floor window overlooks the parking lot from the new, spacious Pastor's office. Situated six feet to the left of the window is Pastor Bart's large wooden desk. A leather couch and chairs extend six feet in front of his desk to accommodate guests. To the left of Bart's desk by an additional six feet is a wardrobe, full-length mirror and mini fridge. Beyond the wardrobe is a private bath-room.

From the window, Bart and Luke watch over the busy parking lot. Luke appears terribly gaunt but he smiles at the sight of happy parishioners in the lot below. He lets out a warm, contented sigh.

Bart grins as he looks over at Luke. In the stark light of the window, Bart suddenly notices how sickly his brother appears. He places an arm around Luke's shoulders.

"They're happy, Luke."

Luke renews his smile. "Yep, they're happy…" He has more to say but hesitates and decides to hold his words.

Bart has something to say as well but, sensing Luke's hesitation, he also chooses to remain quiet. Bart's arm hangs across his older brother's shoulders as the two men stand in awkward silence.

Bart studies Luke as his brother smiles weakly at the window. He decides to speak.

"Hey Luke you don't look so good. Are you feeling alright?"

Luke's eyes drop from the window to his shoes.

"Not really," he answers confusedly. "I'm just sort of tired all the time."

Bart looks genuinely concerned.

"Maybe you should go to the doctor huh?"

Luke shakes his head and looks at Bart.

"I did. He said there was nothing wrong with me and I should just get some rest."

Bart finds it very hard to believe that there's nothing wrong with his brother, but he takes him at his word and makes a joke.

"Well we told the congregation that you were sick when you stepped down, maybe God is punishing you for lying!"

Luke looks dagger-straight at Bart.

"Yeah, *maybe he is.*"

Bart knew it was a bad joke the moment it left his lips. He quickly dismisses it and changes the subject.

"No no no, come on Luke. Hey why don't you and Diane take a nice vacation somewhere?"

Luke looks away from Bart and shakes his head.

"I'm alright, I just need to get more sleep at night."

"Are you sure? You know we have plenty of money, you guys could get away for a little while and warm up somewhere tropical."

Luke musters a reassuring smile and decides to liven things up with a change of topic.

"No really I'm fine Bart! I'd rather be here watching over the church, especially when you guys head out on your honeymoon!"

"A working honeymoon!" Bart protests unconvincingly to his brother. "I've gotta send in regular updates from wherever we're at for the TV guys to roll into the circus shows while I'm gone."

Luke sees right through Bart's phony complaint. He takes a friendly jab at Bart.

"Oh no, I have to keep making money while I'm on *vacation!*"

Called out by his older brother, Bart turns red and laughs. Luke continues teasing him.

"Oh no what will I do!? Money money money oh no!"

Bart breaks into laughter as Luke teases him. Nobody in the world knows Bart like his brother knows him.

The two brothers slap shoulders as Luke steps in front of Bart. He places his hands on Bart's shoulders and looks at him with deep sincerity.

"Bart, there's—"

A knock on the door interrupts Luke as they both look toward the door.

Bart sighs then shouts to the door, "Come in!"

Julie enters. She notices the brothers engaged in a private moment.

"Oh! I can come back!"

Luke looks at Julie and waves her in.

"No no it's fine Julie, come on in!"

Julie knows she interrupted but there's nothing she can do about it now. She enters and closes the door behind her as Luke continues speaking.

"I was just telling Bart good luck today."

Julie and Bart exchange disappointed looks. Fate has deemed the moment lost.

Bart moves forward with life and discusses the day. "There should be some really great energy out there today. You guys wanna know what I have planned?"

Luke laughs as he walks to the door and turns back to Bart.

"Oh no Bart, I don't think I want to know."

Bart wants to get a quick one in on Luke before he leaves.

"I'm gonna start a Jesus chant."

Luke isn't sure if Bart is serious or joking but just to be safe, he plugs his ears and walks out of the room as Julie looks disbelievingly at Bart.

"A Jesus chant," she says flatly. "You're serious?"

Bart laughs to himself, "Yeah."

Julie still isn't sure if Bart is joking. "And how does that work? Wait —haven't I already asked you this before?"

An extremely confident Bart gives it to her straight.

"I'm just gonna go out there and start a Jesus chant."

As Julie tries to envision the impossible, Bart walks over to his wardrobe and pulls out two different jackets. He displays them to Julie for a vote.

"Red or white?"

* * *

A few minutes before 10 a.m., the five-hundred seat church is seated to about seventy percent capacity. Television cameras are in place as the air buzzes with excitement. Donny and the band are still positioned at rear-right but they have much more breathing room on this newer, larger stage.

With Pops still unaccounted for, the band has brought in a new guitarist: a burned-out mid-50s shredder with hair dyed black and cropped short. The band has stepped up their clothing game a bit, with everyone now color-matched to Joey's light-pink dress shirt. To sharper eyes, it would appear that Joey was the lone clothing holdout —the safest path forward for his bandmates would have been matching to him rather than demanding he change colors.

Donny, again wearing his deep burgundy suit and vest, appears recovered from the healing service panic attack. He looks very happy in his new surroundings, bouncing around and checking his notes. For all he knows, maybe Pops hit the lottery and moved to Florida.

Donny looks at the church clock then sits and synchronizes his watch to it. After eyeing his watch for a half minute, he stands and motions for the band's attention. Donny counts them in.

The band hits the mark precisely, playing Bart's theme music as TV cameras pan and tilt near the stage. Donny joyfully teeters to the music before raising the microphone to his lips.

"Brothers and sisters of the *NEW* Salvation Alley Church...Welcome to your new home!"

The congregation applauds and cheers uproariously.

Donny has to shout to be heard, "And please welcome home, your Pastor and mine...*Pastor Bart Baxter!*"

From stage-left, Bart confidently walks out sporting a red jacket and a huge smile. He looks out toward the standing congregation and applauds them. Bart jokingly puts a hand on his brow and squints as he looks out at the sea of people. He walks to the right of the stage and repeats the gesture. The laughing congregation eats it up with applause and whistles.

Bart walks to the pulpit and grabs a handheld wireless microphone placed there. As the music dies out, the applause diminishes and people take their seats.

Smiling, Bart stares out at the congregation for a few seconds as they hush. The silence turns awkward as Bart continues staring out over his quiet congregation. A lone cough, followed by a lone snort, are all that's heard from the pews.

Bart raises the mic to his mouth.

"Jesus," he says quickly.

The congregation laughs uncomfortably. Bart keeps quiet as he looks out at them.

A single deep bullfrog voice calls back to him, "*Amen.*"

Bart ignores the bullfrog. After a few seconds, Bart does it again —this time slower.

"Je–sus."

More uncomfortable laughter, but Bart senses energy building in the congregation as a few more voices call *Amens* back to him.

Then, an individual voice ribbits back.

"Jesus?"

Bart's eyes light up as he points emphatically in the direction of the person calling back correctly. All heads in the congregation turn toward the source—a froggy-looking middle-aged man whose oily face has turned bright red with embarrassment.

Bart does it again, louder this time.

"Jesus!"

A few more voices call back correctly, "Jesus!"

Pastor Bart waves them on. More and more voices now shout correctly but they're out-of-sync with him. Bart continues waving them on as he slows his own voice to synchronize with them. They slowly begin shouting as one.

"Je-sus! Je-sus! Je-sus!"

Bart walks side-to-side, using his arms to lift the congregation to their feet as they all begin chanting together with him. He returns to the pulpit, still chanting and now pumping his fist in the air. Bart steals a glance at Julie. Through laughter, she's chanting too.

The entire congregation is now synchronized, pumping their fists in the air and chanting *Jesus* along with Pastor Bart. Bart makes eye contact with Donny, who was already pumping his arm and chanting. Ever the professional, Donny reads Pastor Bart's look and gets on the mic to add soft vocal support to the chant.

Pastor Bart, at the pulpit, smiles out over his congregation. He's no longer chanting or pumping his fist, instead just smiling and observing in his beautiful red suit. The congregation sees his smile and chants louder, more passionately.

"Je-sus!"

"JE-SUS!"

"JE-SUS!!"

GUM

On weekdays the parking lot at New Salvation Alley Church is typically full of birds. Gulls, crows and pigeons, all minding the pecking order as they take turns picking at candy wrappers and old gum dropped by parishioners who never learned to put trash where it belongs. The birds never mind, in fact they welcome it—to them, it's lunch.

Today, though, is strange. It's Monday but the birds are missing. *All of them.* The only things in the parking lot today are a Cadillac, a Buick, and old gum.

In the office, Luke has a guest chair pulled up alongside Bart's desk. Bart's moved his own chair to sit next to him as they begin reviewing a small stack of papers that Luke's placed on the desk. Bart's desk phone rings and interrupts them.

"Hello?" Bart answers.

A familiar voice is heard through the earpiece—it's Bishop Ronny.

Bart continues, "Yeah Bishop Ronny, what's up?"

From the corner of his eye Bart looks at Luke who's busy gritting his teeth. Bart leans back and turns slightly away from him; he knows Luke doesn't like Ronny, no need to rub it in further with an in-your-face conversation.

"Yes it's this week. This Sunday."

Bishop Ronny's voice is indecipherable through the phone as Bart listens and takes notes.

"Hey Bishop Ronny this is a real bad connection do you want—"

Ronny interrupts and keeps talking. Bart places a finger in his ear and tries very hard to catch the words; it sounds like Bishop Ronny is calling him from the Moon.

"Okay, what's his name?" Bart's own question feeds back annoyingly through the earpiece as he strains to hear. "Bobby McBride? Nope, never heard of him."

Bishop Ronny's voice suddenly rises in the earpiece to perfect clarity, "You never heard of Bobby McBride?"

Bart peeks at Luke to see if he's heard of Bobby McBride. Luke, through gritted teeth, shakes his head and rolls his eyes.

"Nope Bishop Ronny I've never heard of Bobby McBride."

Bishop Ronny utters a high-pitched, garbled exclamation as Bart strains to understand it. Then the phone goes silent.

After a few seconds of silence, Bart sends a message back to the Moon.

"You there, Bishop Ronny?"

Low and barely audible, Bishop Ronny's voice comes through.

"Yeah I'm here."

More silence.

Bart speaks into the silence, "Bishop Ronn—"

Ronny begins speaking again. He gives broken instructions for the next half minute while Bart listens intently and tries to understand what the hell Bishop Ronny is saying.

"Okay sure," Bart replies. "Tell him to come by later this week so we can get acquainted a bit first."

The tone of Bishop Ronny's voice rises in query. Bart does his best to respond accurately to the garbled question.

"What's that? I said tell him—"

Moon-base Ronny interrupts again as Bart plugs his ear tighter. Bart raises his voice to try making himself understood.

"ACQUAINTED. IT MEANS—"

Loud and clear, Bishop Ronny's frustrated voice yells out from the earpiece, "I KNOW WHAT IT MEANS MUTHAFUCKA!"

Luke and Bart look at one another and blink.

"Okay Bishop Ronny just tell him to come by and we'll get him on. Alright. Bye—"

Bishop Ronny hangs up first.

Luke raises inquisitive eyebrows at Bart. Bart fills him in.

"Bishop Ronny is sending one of his guys over to sing for the wedding."

Luke nods sarcastically, "*Ahh…*"

"Some guy named Bobby McBride." Bart looks at Luke and humors him. "Apparently we've been friends for years."

Luke's sarcasm grows, "*AHH…*"

Bart laughs at Luke's reaction but business is business. "Hey I'll take it. If the guy goes over well I'll have him appear in our circus shows while I'm gone."

Changing the subject, Bart nods his head at the small stack of papers on the desk. Luke begins explaining them.

"Okay, this is what you have to choose from." Luke spreads headshots across Bart's desk as he adds sarcastically, "*God help us.*"

Bart studies the headshots from left-to-right. He immediately pounces on a man with a huge perm.

"Who's the sheep?"

Luke leans in to look at the headshot of a man named Stephan Shephard. "That's steh-PON sheh-PARD. He's a musician."

Bart looks confused and points at the name. "That says Stephan."

Luke shakes his head, "He pronounces it steh-PON."

Bart's only on the first circus act and the wind's already left his sails.

"Okay, so what's his gimmick? You said musician?"

Luke nods, "Yeah he plays the keyboards, but here's the thing"—Luke raises a finger to explain a curious detail—"he plays four of them *simultaneously.*"

Bart shakes his head in confusion, "How is that possible?"

Luke turns the headshot over to reveal a full-page color photo of Stephan Shephard, embedded deep within a rectangular jungle of black-and-white piano keys. He's seated spread-eagle with each limb playing a separate keyboard.

Bart is amazed. "He's in! Next."

Luke points to a new headshot as Bart continues staring in awe at Stephan Shephard.

"Okay, this is a big jolly Scottish guy named Cameron MacDonald."

Bart looks over at MacDonald's headshot. "Scottish is good, church people love guys with an accent."

Luke gives Bart a rundown on MacDonald's bio. "This guy raises tons of money for an orphanage he runs in Eastern Europe."

Bart looks suspicious. "Like, orphanages for kids?"

Luke nods and reads from the bio sheet, "Yeah, it says here he operates *multiple girls' orphanages.*"

Bart yells at Luke in shock, "What?!"

Luke is surprised at Bart's reaction. "No good?"

"No, no good at all Luke. That guy's cavorting around with *overseas orphan girls...*"

Bart flips the headshot over to reveal a picture of big, jolly Cameron MacDonald, surrounded by soulless, unsmiling orphans. Bart immediately winces in disgust.

Luke looks at the photo. On second glance, he sees Cameron MacDonald for the predator he is. He pulls the photo away as Bart vigorously shakes the disgust from his head.

"Okay, moving on to..." Luke fishes through the remains of his stack and finds a new headshot to place in the mix. "Yakov Smirnoff."

Bart sits up and blinks in wonderment at Luke.

"Yakov Smirnoff?"

Luke nods and shows the headshot to Bart—it's Yakov Smirnoff alright.

"Yes Bart, Yakov Smirnoff. He has a family-friendly comedy routi—"

"We're talking about the *same guy* right?" Bart still doesn't believe what he's being told.

"Bart, there's only *one* Yakov Smirnoff. Look!" Luke points again at the headshot as Bart studies it. It is *undeniably* Yakov Smirnoff.

"The guy's a huge hit in the Midwest, Bart. You have to buy tickets months in advance for his Branson shows."

Bart finally accepts the facts. "Okay he's in!" Bart happily confirms.

A polite triple knock on the door interrupts them. Bart and Luke look at each other confused—they didn't expect anyone.

Bart hollers to the door, "Come in!"

The door cracks open and an extremely timid Donny pokes his head in.

"Hi Pastor Bart…Pastor Luke…"

Bart appears mildly annoyed at the interruption. Luke takes the lead.

"Hey Donny, how can we help you?" Luke says flatly.

Donny continues poking his head through the door as he replies in a high, timid voice, "I wondered if I could have a word with Pastor Bart?"

Bart quickly looks down at the headshots. He's now really annoyed at Donny's interruption and responds curtly, "What is it Donny?"

Without being invited in, Donny proceeds to squeeze his entire enormous body through the barely open door. Once inside, he awkwardly closes the door behind him. Luke can feel the heat coming off Bart as Donny continues with his clumsy interruption. Luke feels terrible for Donny and by the looks of it, things are only going to get worse for him.

Donny continues in his high, timid voice, "Well *Bart,* umm…"

Bart, looking down at the table, blink his eyes closed as Luke cringes inside. Every move Donny makes is wrong.

"…since we're in the new church now and are on TV and everything, I was wondering if I might ask…"

Luke drops his head and whispers to himself, *"Don't do it Donny."*

"…for a little pay increase?"

Luke closes his eyes tightly. He did it.

Donny smiles nervously at Bart who continues looking down at his desk. Luke is leaning forward in his chair, elbows on his knees while he looks at his hands.

Bart raises his head, looks at Donny and flatly rephrases his question. "You mean a raise?"

Donny smiles at Pastor Bart and nods his head gently. "Yeah, that's—yeah, uh-huh."

Bart's voice turns slightly sharp, "And *why* do you think you deserve a raise, *Donny?*"

Donny isn't prepared for the question; this wasn't how the scenario played out last week in his head. He fumbles an answer. "Well, I suppose that I've, umm, played a part in helping us get to this beautiful new church, and the umm, TV—"

Bart starts laughing; Luke wants to vanish.

Bart looks over at Luke, currently frozen in place and looking at his hands. Then he looks up at Donny and continues laughing. Donny is fast becoming unsettled as Bart stands up from his desk.

"You know Donny, I think I liked you better when you called me *Pastor* Bart."

Donny now realizes this is turning very bad. He watches as Bart paces around behind is desk.

"The guy who called me Pastor Bart that very first day...that guy *knew who was in charge.*"

Bart continues pacing.

"The guy who called me Pastor Bart, he knew that there was"—Bart raises a finger in emphasis—*"a distance,"* Bart pauses to stare coldly at Donny, "between us both."

Donny raises his hand to speak but Bart shakes his head at him.

"Do you know what your role is here, *Donny?*"

Donny thinks about it and begins to respond when Bart cuts him off.

"Let me *tell you* your role."

Donny stands silent near the door.

Pointing, Bart tells him, "You're the *fat guy.*"

Donny is taken aback as Bart resumes pacing.

"You're the *fat guy* who talks to the crowd before the show and sings a song every once in awhile."

Donny can't believe what he's hearing.

"And do you know how many *fat guys* are out there who can *do your job, Donny?*"

Bart stops pacing and looks directly at Donny.

"Millions."

The room is dead silent.

Bart resumes his pacing.

"So in answer to your question, *Donny,* no. No you cannot have a raise."

Bart fires off one more volley.

"And if you think you played anything more than a *negligible* part in making this church what it is today, then you are *mistaken."*

Bart looks condescendingly at Donny. "You know what negligible means, right? It means *in-sig-ni-fi-cant."*

Donny explodes in a high screech, "SHAME ON YOU! SHAME ON YOU BART BAXTER!" He points at Bart, "YOU ARE A BAD MAN!"

Bart crosses his arms and watches Donny's outburst.

"I RISKED MY LIFE FOR THIS CHURCH! YOU DON'T KNOW WHAT GOES ON IN THE BAND!"

Bart dismisses him with a snide nod, *"I'll learn."*

Donny looks to Luke who's still frozen looking at his hands. He points again at Bart and screeches, "YOU ARE A BAD MAN BART BAXTER! YOU ARE NOT GOOD, YOU ARE BAD! SHAME ON YOU!"

Pressing his palms downward, Bart tries to quiet Donny down with a sarcastic shush.

"NO! SHAME ON YOU! YOU ARE NO MAN OF GOD! HOW DARE YOU CALL YOURSELF A PASTOR!"

Donny's eyes grow wide as he looks at Bart's Bible on the desk. *"HOW DARE YOU HOLD THAT BIBLE!"*

Luke cocks his head sideways at Donny's comment.

Donny furiously opens the door and slams it as he walks out, leaving the room silent. Stomps are heard through the floor as Donny storms out of the building.

Luke is very, very annoyed at Bart's treatment of Donny. A simple *no* would have worked, or even a *yes*—they have plenty of money to go around.

Luke breaks the silence. "That wasn't cool, Bart."

Bart has no response as he moves to the window to watch for Donny's exit to the parking lot.

"Seriously Bart…" Luke looks at Bart, whose back is turned to him as he looks out the window. Bart doesn't want to face Luke's criticism. *"Not cool."*

Bart watches through the office window as Donny angrily stomps out to a small white Ford Fiesta. He yanks on the locked door, which yanks him back. Donny hits the alarm key to unlock the door then opens it wide.

Before getting in, Donny looks up at the tinted window that Bart stands behind and flips the bird.

Bart's pleasantly surprised by Donny standing up for himself. "Nice, Donny!" he remarks loudly.

With Bart's back turned to him, Luke looks back down at his hands and shakes his head. Bart watches as Donny tears out of the parking lot in his tiny white car.

Friends & Family

Flowers and carnations are seen on lapels as formally dressed parishioners happily glide through a nearly full parking lot toward the church. The church sign reads:

> *Join us for the wedding of Pastor Bart and Julie Baxter! This Sunday 10am. Special Guest Bobby McBride!*

Big John and Rich wear carnations on their tightly thighed suits while greeting incoming parishioners at the door.

Inside, television cameramen make adjustments as excited parishioners drop thick envelopes into two large boxes labeled:

MR AND MRS BART BAXTER SAY: WE LOVE YOU!

The band members wear light-pink suits with white carnations, including Joey, whose jacket has tails. A new singer has replaced Donny. Like Donny, the new singer is very overweight, but whereas Donny had dark brown hair, the new singer's hair is bright red. He bounces around and hums to himself preshow just like Donny and appears to be just as nervous.

Mrs Evans and two older parishioners discuss the singer.

"That's not Donny?" Mrs Evans inquires.

"No Grace that's a different guy, he just looks like him," answers Margaret, eighty-five years old and sharp as a tack.

Nancy, seventy years old and wearing a carnation freshly cut from her garden, raises reading glasses to her eyes to inspect the new singer. She makes a positive id.

"That's Donny."

Mrs Evans nods to her, "It is, right?"

Margaret shakes her head. "Ladies, I'm telling you that's not Donny. Donny had beautiful brown hair, this guy is a redhead."

Mrs Evans is growing frustrated with Margaret's insistence on bursting her bubble. She shrugs her arms, "Well maybe he dyed it?"

Nancy quickly agrees with Mrs Evans, "You're right Grace he dyed it!" A garden spider hunkers down unnoticed inside her carnation.

Margaret is becoming exasperated trying to convince the stubborn ladies that the new singer is not Donny.

"No Grace, you can't dye your hair that color."

Mrs Evans opens her eyes wide at Margaret and points to the singer as evidence, "Well HE did!"

* * *

In the office, Bart has just put the finishing touches on his wedding tuxedo and looks himself over in the mirror. Luke relaxes in Bart's desk chair, looking fondly at his little brother. Luke's health appears to be improving.

"Alright so you'll have everything under control while I'm gone?" Bart asks.

Luke reassures him, "Bart, I got it."

Bart presses to make sure. "Okay because once we leave today, we're gone. The plane leaves in six hours."

Luke waves him off. "*I've got it* Bart, just relax and enjoy your big day."

Bart smiles and walks over to Luke. His eyes soften in sincerity.

"Luke, hey I'm sorry I got you sucked into all this stuff."

Luke is surprised by the left field comment.

"What stuff?"

Bart searches his mind for a way to describe it. He puts his arms out to encompass their present surroundings.

"Just, you know, all of this. All the money stuff and, you know... *not a lot of God.*"

Luke shakes his head and laughs at Bart.

"Bart, I'm a big boy. I could have told you no when you offered to take the church. I could have walked away when we got the check from Mrs Christianson!"

Bart hadn't considered that.

Luke laughs again. "I could have told you no when you wanted that stupid suit sent to you in prison!"

This time, Bart laughs too. "Hey do you know what I had to *do* to keep that suit safe!?"

Luke waves Bart off and shakes his head. "No no you told me already, I don't wanna hear it again."

Bart stops laughing and again speaks sincerely, "Okay. I just want you to know that I'm sorry for being me sometimes."

"It's alright Bart. You're my brother, I understand."

Luke places an arm around Bart's shoulder as Bart reciprocates. The two boys smile.

"Okay let's get you married!"

* * *

A familiar living room television is tuned to the *Blessed Flock Network* as a grandfather clock dings the hour.

On-screen, Bart's theme music plays as quick clips of Pastor Bart's healing service are shown. Donny's old show introduction, owned by Bart until he decides to stop using it, provides the initial voice-over as a graphic simultaneously appears:

"Welcome to *God's Alive! With Pastor Bart Baxter!*"

Bart's theme music quickly fades out and is replaced by an organ playing "Here Comes The Bride". An advertisement begins as an overlay is displayed at the bottom of the screen:

Call us NOW! 888-LIV-HEAL

Own Pastor Baxter's *WEDDING DVD!*

$50 – Ask for 'WEDDING LOVE GIFT'

Video is shown of Bart and Julie on stage with Luke presiding behind them. The new red-haired singer, also tenor-voiced, provides a fresh voice-over to accompany the video:

"In the presence of God, Pastor Bart and Julie joined themselves in holy union…"

A closeup shows a comically shaky-handed Bart receiving the wedding ring from Luke. Cut to a new closeup of Julie's hand, also shaking ridiculously hard, as she spreads her fingers to receive the ring. As Bart prepares to place the ring on Julie's finger, the scene quickly fades to white.

Video suddenly appears of the new singer bouncing around and singing happily as the band rocks. Joey scowls in the background while playing bass. Balloons and confetti rain down on a celebrating congregation as the new singer continues his voice-over:

"Were you there? Did you see it? Live it *all over again* with your fifty-dollar wedding love gift!

"And, if you never received your wedding invitation, *good news!* The phones are still open to receive your *free* personalized wedding invitation, with wedding gift of a hundred dollars or more!"

At screen bottom, the overlay changes to reflect the new offer:

Pastor Baxter's *WEDDING DVD w/ LIMITED EDITION PERSONALIZED INVITE!*

$100 or more – Ask for 'WEDDING GIFT'

The two offer names are confusingly similar. That's intentional, since anyone charged more will *never* call to complain—they most likely won't even realize it.

As "Here Comes The Bride" continues playing, a tacky clipart wedding invitation is displayed on-screen:

-BY SPECIAL INVITE ONLY- (Your Name Here) is warmly invited to join Pastor Bart and Julie as they become one in the presence of God and (Your Name Here)

More voice over from the new singer:

"See the bride walk down the aisle!"

Teaser video is shown of the congregation rising to their feet before Julie enters the aisle. The video cuts just before Julie begins her walk.

"See the wedding vows!"

Teaser video is shown of a shaky Bart, desperately trying to cry real tears while reading his vows to a lip-biting Julie.

"Plus, a special performance by the one and only *Bobby McBride!*"

Video is shown of the man known as Bobby McBride singing to Bart and Julie. Bart, pouty-faced, holds his hands out in thanks toward his *good friend* Bobby. Again, Julie bites her lip to keep from laughing.

"Love lost. Kids grown. Many things in life have a way of *getting away from us.*"

Video is shown of Bart's Cadillac in the parking lot, full of streamers and with *Just Married* temporarily painted on the side. From the driver's seat, Bart waves and smiles obnoxiously at the mass of people applauding him in the parking lot.

Slowly, the car begins to turn away from the camera. The cameraman gets a view of the rear, now displaying a vanity license plate reading *REBORN.*

As Bart's car pulls away from the camera, the voice-over implores viewers:

"Don't-let-this-one…*get away!*"

Master & Servant

A montage begins to Depeche Mode's "Personal Jesus"—

Bart and Julie, wearing cheap sunglasses and big smiles, tow luggage behind them as they walk into the departure terminal of Los Angeles International Airport.

On the BFN channel, *God's Alive! With Pastor Bart Baxter!* plays clips of Bart's live healings at the old church.

Bart and Julie clink champagne glasses together and laugh from their seats in First Class.

Bobby McBride sings to Bart's swooning congregation as Pastor Luke double-checks his hair in a backstage mirror.

Bart and Julie arrive at the airport in Monte Carlo.

An elderly hand dials a telephone as a credit card rests on the phone stand.

In closeup, Stephan Shephard's permed hair shakes. The camera pulls back to reveal him working his hands up and down the keyboards.

Bart and Julie open a hotel room door to reveal their opulent suite at the *Resort Fantastique.*

Returning to Stephan Shephard's hands on the keys, the camera now pulls further away to reveal him also holding down chords with his feet. He looks triumphantly at the congregation, who applaud happily and nod their heads. One man leans to his wife, points at Stephan Shephard and mouths the words, *"He's good!"*

"Personal Jesus" dies down low as the montage pauses.

* * *

At the resort pool, Bart grabs a seat next to an older tattooed man wearing designer shades while sunbathing quietly in a lounge chair. The man's entire body is slathered in oil and his junk is under arrest by a speedo. On the table next to him rests a half-full cocktail glass and a bottle of baby oil.

As Bart lies back in the hot sun, the man lazily looks over at him.

"Preacher?" the man asks in an English accent.

Perplexed by the Englishman's accurate guess, Bart looks at him and laughs.

"How can you tell?"

The Englishman shifts his head an extra millimeter in Bart's direction—he doesn't want to be rude.

"We learn to recognize one another."

Bart grins at the cool Englishman. "Bart Baxter," he says while offering his hand.

"Dave." The Englishman halfheartedly raises an arm to accept the handshake but the rest of his body barely moves. The sun is just *too nice* out here.

The Englishman slowly returns to gazing straight ahead. Ice shifts in his cocktail glass.

"So what's your specialty, Bart?"

"Healing," Bart replies semi-seriously.

The Englishman hazily tilts his head towards Bart.

"Ah," he says with feigned surprise.

Bart likes the Englishman's dryness. He offers up another skill from his résumé.

"And sometimes I sing."

The Englishman replies with the same subdued reaction.

"Ah."

Bart returns the question—this Englishman seems friendly enough. "And you?"

The Englishman laughs slightly. He rubs his oily hands together and turns them palms out in front of him to illustrate.

"Healer."

Bart laughs out loud at the coincidence.

Seizing the opportunity, the Englishman turns his head to look fully at Bart.

"And sometimes I sing."

Bart laughs hysterically at the mysterious Englishman. The Englishman joins in with tired, sun-beaten laughter while lifting his cocktail glass to Bart.

"Cheers!"

* * *

"Personal Jesus" resumes as the montage continues—

Bart and Julie, both *very* tan and wearing designer shades, arrive at a French airport terminal bound for Japan.

As a television shows the ad for Bart and Julie's wedding video, an elderly hand grabs the phone once again.

Inside Bart's office, Luke builds stacks of cash and checks.

Tan Bart and Julie are hounded by rabid fans and flashing cameras in a Japanese airport.

In a formal Japanese church ceremony, Pastor Bart is presented with a ceremonial Japanese Bible.

In the same church, Bart is presented with a ceremonial kimono.

Then he's presented with a ceremonial karate gi—

—and a ceremonial samurai sword.

Yakov Smirnoff delivers his catchphrase *"What a country!"* as Bart's congregation laughs hysterically.

In Bart's office, Luke is overwhelmed as he continues stacking cash, checks and coinage higher and higher. Opened envelopes litter the floor.

Crowds of identically clothed Japanese men and women fill the stage as Bart delivers a passionate healing sermon.

On stage, Pastor Bart screams wildly at a Japanese man clothed in black pants, white shirt and black tie. Bart strikes the air in front of the man's face and he falls to the ground with a great flourish. Other worshippers on stage—untouched by Bart—follow the man's lead, dramatically waving their arms as they fall off to the side.

A new Japanese man clambers onto the stage. From roughly ten feet away, Pastor Bart uses his finger to zero in on the man and shoot him *right between the eyes*. The man's head snaps back and he falls into the arms of the congregation, healed.

The stacks of money in Bart's office are now comically high. Try as he might, Luke can't stack it any higher.

Pastor Bart, eyes-wild at his Japanese pulpit, holds a Bible aloft and screams at the congregation. Surrounding him, a sea of black-haired worshippers cower and cover their heads to shelter themselves from Pastor Bart's almighty power—in this live-action roleplay, *Bart is their God*.

Back in Bart's office, a very frustrated Luke now resorts to throwing money haphazardly on the office floor.

It's early morning in a park painted forest-green as Bart, clad in his ceremonial karate gi, performs katas. Beyond Bart, an expansive sky shimmers blue. On that shimmering sky, a magnificent red sun rises.

Locks Magnetic

As Pastor Bart Baxter climbs the stairs toward his office, he tries to remember the dream he had the night before that bothered him so much. He remembers sheep appearing, lots of sheep, and his father was there yelling at him about something.

Unable to remember the bothersome dream, Bart writes it off to airplane food and jet lag as he approaches his office door. He unlocks the door and opens it to find bills, coins and checks stacked and strewn everywhere. Bart can't believe his eyes.

* * *

By late morning, Bart has cleaned up the office. All currency is packed into cardboard boxes on the floor as Bart reviews church financials on his desk computer. A key unlocks the office door and in walks Luke, looking fresh as a daisy.

"So I see you've cleaned up?" Luke asks jokingly.

Bart smiles broadly.

Luke looks around and notices a person missing. "Where's Julie?"

Bart happily explains, "All the church stuff in Japan burned her out so I told her to get away for awhile. She's in Colorado with her sister for the next month looking for vacation homes. And skiing."

"Julie can ski?" Luke inquires with a laugh.

"She's taking lessons."

Luke looks at the cash-filled cardboard boxes then sits down in front of Bart's desk. "Hey a guy's coming in on Wednesday to install better locks on the doors, one of those magnetic things. It buzzes, I figured you'd like that."

Bart nods then looks back at his computer.

Luke expected more enthusiasm from him, especially after mentioning the buzzer. He tries again.

"I figured since this is becoming a mini bank vault, a little extra security wouldn't hurt."

Bart again just nods. Luke can tell something is bugging him.

"Bart, what's up?"

Bart leans back in his chair and thinks through a response. Luke gives him time to work through his thoughts.

Bart sits up. "You know Luke, I don't feel like I worked for all this money. Japan was only two nights of shows, after that it was all sightseeing and comp'd sushi. Where's the challenge in that?"

Bart turns in his chair to look out the window.

"It's just too easy to take their money, Luke."

Luke listens. He knows Bart has always loved a challenge, but it seems that there's more going on here than him being bummed out because making money is *too easy.*

"Sometimes I feel dirty about it—not a lot, just a little. But that gets drowned out by the excitement I feel when I take it. And they love me for it, Luke.

Bart turns back and looks at Luke.

"They love me for *taking their money.*"

Luke's figured his brother out now. It's not the ease with which he makes his money, it's *how* he makes his money. That's good, because Luke has already given this a lot of thought. A *lot* of thought.

Luke offers counsel to his little brother. "You know what Bart? What is it you said to me way back in the beginning of all this? That you entertain people, and they pay you for it?"

Bart's ears perk up in attention. "Right," he nods.

Luke continues, "Well, maybe the money doesn't matter in the grand scheme of things. Whether you spend their money or they do, in the long run *it's just paper with a guy's face printed on it.*"

Bart listens intently to each word coming from his brother.

"Maybe what really matters is that you're giving these people a thrill. Joy, laughter and tears...You're giving them all of that, Bart. You're giving them a reason to *feel.*"

Luke presses the full meaning from his words, *"You're giving them life*, Bart."

Luke's words strike a chord in Bart. Not a chord of emotion; rather, a chord of self-awareness.

"So when all is said and done, maybe it's not so wrong for you to take their money if they end up being happier people because of it."

Bart smiles at his brother. He can certainly get behind Luke's justification of the Bart Baxter business model.

Luke adds, "I mean, *I wouldn't* do what you do."

Bart tilts his head back and laughs.

"And you *definitely* need to stop being such an asshole to people."

Bart laughs again but Luke is serious.

"What you did to Donny wasn't cool man."

Bart acknowledges with a small nod to himself, "Yeah maybe I was —"

"No, not maybe, Bart!" Luke insists. "That wasn't cool, Donny was a good guy."

Bart smiles at his brother, "You're right."

"Okay." Satisfied that his job as counselor is complete, Luke gets up and heads for the door. "I'm gonna go and let you build a house out of gold bricks in here."

Bart looks at the boxes full of cash and laughs. He hollers at Luke, "Do you know how much we made?"

Luke doesn't look back as he grabs the door, "I don't want to know."

Bart responds jokingly, "Well it was *a lot!*"

Luke opens the door and looks back at Bart.

"You made it Bart. Not me."

Bart's always envisioned the two of them as a team, but Luke's words make his own position clear—Bart is the true star of this show.

Before Luke exits he reminds Bart, "Don't forget that guy's coming for the locks on Wednesday." Luke points at the boxes of money on the floor, "You might wanna do something with those."

Bart looks at the boxes, "Yeah I got it."

The door closes as Bart stares at dollar amounts on the computer screen, his mind preoccupied with his brother's kind words.

* * *

Later that night, Bart walks to his car in the vacant church parking lot. As he approaches the driver's side he notices an envelope wedged under the front wheel. Leaning down to inspect it more closely, he sees words written in all-caps on the front:

PASTOR BAXTER PLEASE HELP

Puzzled, Bart picks up the envelope. He sits down in the driver's seat and opens it. Inside he finds a small piece of paper:

Big Bad Wolf,

This ticket is good for one free ride. Tonight only. I'm in a red car on the street outside Bishop Ronnys. We go wherever you want to go. No cameras, no spies. Just me and you.

Nobody knows you like I do.

Little Red Riding Hood

The tempting letter visibly upsets Bart. He stares aimlessly through the window in deep thought. Bart reads the letter again, then looks down and sighs heavily.

He angrily slams his arm against the passenger seat, "Fuck!"

* * *

Across the street from Bishop Ronny's compound, a red compact car is parked in the shadowy area between two streetlamps. A few cars speed by in opposite directions, briefly silhouetting an unknown figure inside the car.

A white Cadillac, driving slower than normal traffic, approaches parallel to the red car. The Cadillac slows to a stop next to the car, pauses briefly, then speeds away. A moment later, the red car's headlights flick on. The vehicle and its occupant drive off in pursuit of the Cadillac.

* * *

The new magnetic lock has been installed on the office door. An unlock button is installed underneath Bart's desktop, plus a button on the wall next to the door for guests to press when they leave. As the installer explained to Bart the day before, pressing the button unlocks the door for five seconds and, in the current configuration, nobody enters or leaves without one of the buttons being pressed. Only people with access cards can change the configuration—those people are Bart and Luke.

Bart's having fun making the lock buzz while he reviews the many different locking configurations shown in the owner's manual.

Brrrr.

"Luke, it says it has a 'Vault Mode' where both cards have to be swiped to get in and out. Do we want that?"

Luke's busy setting up a new computer monitor on Bart's desk.

"No Bart, that's a bad idea. What if one of the cards stops wor—"

Brrrr. Bart interrupts Luke with the buzzer.

Mildly annoyed, Luke laughs it off and continues. "If one of the cards stops working then we have no way to get out."

Bart thinks about that for a second.

"But why would a card stop working?" Bart asks.

"Because these guys were the cheapest installers I foun—"

Brrrr.

Luke's really annoyed now. "Dude enou—"

Brrrrrrrrrrrrr.

Luke stares at Bart with extreme displeasure at getting buzzed. "Bart, STOP!"

Bart suddenly remembers his dream from the other night, the one that bothered him so much.

He was in a large grassy field, surrounded by a large flock of sheep with human faces. The faces were of people in his congregation. Bart wasn't scared because the sheep weren't hostile. In fact, they were taking turns eating from his hands. His hands, however, were empty —the sheep were quite happily munching on air.

A sheep with the sex-addicted woman's face on it began vigorously licking Bart's palms. Crowding in next to her were two sheep with the faces of Mrs Evans and the Headache Woman. These sheep also began licking his palms as Bart watched in amazement.

Suddenly, the Mrs Evans sheep raised its docked tail and began shitting gold coins. Bart was awestruck as coins plinked down from the rear of Mrs Evans.

The Mrs Evans sheep began calling out to the flock, *"Baaah! Baaah!"*

The other sheep copied the behavior of Mrs Evans, raising their tails to poop gold coins as they joined into a chorus of *baaahs*. Small mounds of gold soon littered the landscape as Bart's amazement grew.

In the distance, Bart noticed two rams trot down from a small grassy hill and begin plodding curiously toward the flock. The rams wore the faces of church doormen Big John and Rich, and Bart remembers that the rams had enormous testicles. Bart had no fear of the rams—he was just impressed by the size of their balls.

Abruptly, a voice yelled out, "STOP!"

Bart looked to the source of the voice and saw his father, Pastor James Baxter, standing on a different, larger hilltop. Next to his father was Mrs Christianson, alive and well and completely bald. In her hand was a cattle-prod, energized and snapping at the air. Mrs Christianson was very aggressively chewing gum and glaring at Bart.

Bart returned his attention to the flock of gold-pooping sheep and suddenly found himself surrounded by huge piles of sheep manure. The gold had turned to shit and Bart was stuck in the middle of it.

Bart looked back for his father on the hilltop, but he was gone. Only Mrs Christianson remained.

Suddenly, Mrs Christianson began running toward Bart. She ran powerfully, determined, like an all-pro linebacker gunning for a rookie quarterback. With her cattle-prod in hand, she chomped down tight on her chewing gum and came right for him. Two hundred feet quickly shrank to a hundred, then fifty feet as Mrs Christianson closed the distance on him. Bart set his jaw and braced himself for the collision—*this is gonna hurt*, he thought to himself.

Just before impact, Bart awoke from the dream with his jaw in pain from grinding his teeth.

"Bart, what did you want to show me?" Luke is finished setting up the new monitor.

Bart shakes off the dream and snaps himself back to the present. He looks at the monitor.

"The volume is up on this thing right?" Bart asks.

Luke searches for the volume button on the monitor. After navigating some on-screen menus, he finds the volume and turns it up.

Bart double-clicks a file on his desktop and a video begins to play. He smiles and points at the monitor.

"Check it out Luke it's me in Japan!"

A newly produced episode of *God's Alive! With Pastor Bart Baxter!* plays on the monitor. The episode begins with a very tan Bart saying hello to the camera in stilted Japanese:

"Ko-nee-chee-wa brothers and sisters!"

Bart laughs upon seeing himself.

Luke notices Bart's extreme bronze coloring. "Were you really that color or do I need to return the monitor?"

Bart shakes his head with a confident smile, "That's *healthy,* Luke."

Luke disagrees, "It looks like you sat under a heat lamp at Dennys for a few hours."

Bart's confident smile turns triumphant.

"Godlike, Luke. The Japanese *loved* it."

A knock on the door surprises Bart and Luke. They look at each other in confusion, neither knowing who would be coming by on a Thursday.

Not wanting to further upset Luke, Bart looks to him for authorization to hit the buzzer. Luke gives him a nod and Bart hits it.

Brrrr.

The door opens. In walks Grace, Bishop Ronny's secretary, dressed in a red pantsuit and carrying a briefcase. Bart's eyes shoot lightning bolts at her as Luke is confused by the unknown woman.

"May we help you?" Luke asks.

Grace responds coyly to Luke, "Uhhh..." She pauses, then looks at Bart and smiles.

"Bart can."

Luke is still confused as he looks at Bart, who appears ready to jump over the desk and murder this mystery girl. Bart peeks over at Luke and catches himself.

Luke connects the dots. "Bart?" he asks disappointedly.

Bart shakes his head in dismissal but Luke sees right through him.

Disgusted, Luke walks to the door and presses the wall-mounted button next to it.

Brrrr.

Luke angrily opens the door and leaves.

Bart's eyes burn furiously at Grace as she nonchalantly approaches his desk with briefcase in hand.

"So how you doing, *big bad wolf?*" she asks sarcastically.

Bart's fists clench as he instantly becomes enraged.

Grace wisely backs off her teasing. "So here's what I want Bart," she says matter-of-factly.

She places her briefcase on Bart's desk and begins to open it. Grace is rattled by the white-hot anger boiling off him, but she's in too deep to leave now.

"A hundred thousand dollars plus—"

Bart grabs the unlatched briefcase and throws it against the door. "YOU DON'T GET MY MONEY BITCH!"

Black-and-white photographs of Bart and Grace in a motel parking lot fly from the briefcase as it slams against the door. Grace freezes in fear as Bart slowly approaches from behind his desk.

Bart spits venom, "Do you really think I would build this church into a masterpiece, a *diamond*, simply to give my money away to a piece of shit gutter slut like you?"

Bart puffs up as Grace begins to retreat.

"Do you really think I would give you *my* money so you can spend it on hairspray and bubblegum and whatever the fuck else you waste your money on?"

Bart menacingly walks Grace down as she now quickly retreats to the door, eyes wide with fear.

"Do you even know who you're talking to, little girl?"

Grace reaches the door and pulls on it but it won't open. As Bart approaches her, she cowers in fear.

Grace breathlessly warns Bart, "Don't touch me or I'll scream."

Bart stares at her neck and tells her threateningly, "If you scream, *I'll touch you.*"

Grace is frozen in place as Bart slowly paces away from her. He calms down as the distance between them grows.

"You see those people in my church every Sunday, Grace? They are *mine*. They worship *me*. God sets the rules and his congregation follows those rules, or else they suffer His wrath."

Bart raises his hands and mimics a sermon, "Ladies and gentleman, we're all wearing red next week."

From a distance, Bart turns and faces Grace.

"And next week, Grace, all I see as I look out on my congregation is a beautiful sea of red while a thousand pathetic little eyeballs look to me for approval."

Bart slowly approaches her. Anger builds with each step.

"If I tell them I'm angry, Grace, they'll do anything to appease me. *Woe is she who curses God.*"

Bart positions himself directly in Grace's face as she trembles in fear.

"In this church, I am the way, the truth and the light."

Bart lowers his voice to a menacing whisper, "In this church, *I am God and you are nothing.*"

He stares darkly at Grace as she cowers below him.

Bart pounds the button on the wall.

Brrrr.

Bart threatens Grace with his eyes. "Now get the fuck outta my church."

Grace quickly grabs her briefcase and runs out the door. Bart stares at the pictures scattered on the floor and sighs heavily.

Revelation

In Julie's house, Bart unfolds the local weekend paper as he drinks his morning coffee. On the front page he sees his picture accompanied by the headline he was dreading:

Popular Televangelist accused by Mistress

The smaller sub-headline reads:

He said he would kill me if I told anyone, says Mistress

Below and to the right of the main story, a smaller headline goes unnoticed by Bart:

Man's body found—Silky Strangler suspected

The first line of the Strangler story reads:

"The remains of a man known affectionately to friends as 'Pops' have been found..."

Bart puts the paper down and turns on the television. The local TV news is in the middle of covering the story. Pictures of Pastor Bart Baxter appear as a male reporter provides voice-over:

"Ms Anderson says that she and Pastor Baxter have had an ongoing, months-long romance—"

Bart stares unblinking at the screen.

"—which ended abruptly when she learned he was married."

Bart's in deep thought as the story continues. Grace appears on-screen speaking to a reporter:

"'I told him I didn't think it was right that we see each other any-more if he's married—'"

Bart strokes his neck under the chin as he continues thinking.

"'—and that's when he threatened me.'"

Bart's eyes are frozen to the TV as he pulls at his chin, trying to figure a way out of his predicament.

More images of Pastor Bart Baxter are shown as the reporter con-tinues his voice-over:

"Ms Anderson alleges that Pastor Baxter threatened to, quote, strangle her, if she told anyone about—"

Bart clicks the TV off. A text message arrives on his cell phone. It's from Julie.

> You have three days to get your shit out of my house.
> Keep your fucking money. Goodbye forever.

Bart puts the phone down and slowly sips his coffee. He strokes his neck again as he works his way through this mental maze.

His cellphone rings. Bishop Ronny's name is displayed by caller ID. Bart takes a breath and answers the phone without a word.

"Bart, please tell me you didn't mess with that bitch?"

Silence.

"I fired her ass weeks ago man. I thought you knew that?"

Silence.

"You gotta make this right, Bart. You can't just get walked on by that bitch, you gotta make it right man."

Bart utters his first words. "I'm going live tomorrow morning."

Bishop Ronny responds with surprise, "Live, you sure? Just put out a taped message or someth—"

"LIVE Ronny!" Bart demands.

The conversation pauses as Ronny thinks about Bart's demand.

"Alright, live it is. You want me to send—"

Bart hangs up first.

Stroking his neck, Bart stares in silence at the blank television screen.

* * *

Luke's leaning against his Buick as Bart parks next to him in the desolate church parking lot. Bart exits the car and Luke joins him on the walk to the office. Two reporters appear out of nowhere.

"Pastor Baxter do you have any comment on the—"

"Guys," Bart smiles as he interrupts, "please feel free to attend our service this morning."

The reporters continue pressing, "Pastor Baxter do you have a mistre—"

"Guys!" Bart smiles again. "Attend the service and you'll get everything you want. Otherwise, I'll have you barred from entering the building and you'll get nothing."

The reporters consider the offer, then agree and walk away.

Bart shouts toward them, "And don't go harassing my congregation!"

Luke looks haggard again. Very haggard and very worried. He walks with Bart toward the rear entrance as his front hair dangler flops down onto his face. Luke brushes it back with his hand.

"So what's the plan Bart?"

Bart tells Luke plainly, "I'm throwing a Hail Mary and we'll see if anyone catches it."

Luke doesn't look very convinced. He changes topics.

"Julie?"

Bart shakes his head regretfully as Luke sighs.

"Okay, well just tell me what you need today and I'll do it." Luke puts his hand on Bart's shoulder for reassurance. There's not much else he can do since Bart's done this to himself. But, Bart is still his brother and he'll do what he can to support him.

The two men continue walking toward the office when Bart suddenly stops and looks down—he's stepped in gum.

Bart looks at his shoe and swears angrily, *"Goddamn it!"*

* * *

Blustery winds begin swirling as the parking lot fills. Attendance at New Salvation Alley is high as usual, but churchgoers are not joyous today. Reassuring hugs are offered in the parking lot and some are openly crying. A slow, depressed mass marches on toward the church, passing a church sign that reads:

Special Message from Pastor Bart Baxter. Today 10am.

Through the office window, sunlight is sporadically dimmed by rain clouds as Bart and Luke go over final details.

Luke informs Bart, "I told the doormen and ushers to keep the reporters seated in the back and quiet."

Bart nods.

"And the wireless mic isn't working so you gotta use the wired one at the pulpit."

Bart grits his teeth. "Brand new church and the mics aren't working already," he says sarcastically.

Luke tries to add levity, "Well I know today isn't the day for jokes, but the wired one didn't work either."

Bart sighs in discouragement.

"We worked it out though, one of the music guys ran a fresh mic cable and it works now. But watch your step, he had to run it over the stage so we covered it with a mat behind the pulpit."

Bart tries to joke, "That's fine, I don't plan on doing any dancing today."

His own joke fails him and he sighs again.

Luke puts a hand on Bart's shoulder. "I'm going out there now. Is there anything else you need before I go?"

Bart looks at Luke for a second, then hugs him. Luke is surprised at the initiation but returns the hug warmly.

"I love you Luke."

"I love you too, Bart."

* * *

The congregation is dead silent as Luke takes his seat up front. He bows his head and prays.

* * *

Bart's panting heavily as he enters the office bathroom to look at himself in the mirror—he's almost lost his nerve. He clasps his hands in prayer and looks upwards, then quickly dismisses the act as futile with a *pfft* and a hand wave. He looks again in the mirror, takes a deep breath, and steels himself for what's to come.

* * *

The clock hits ten. Pastor Bart Baxter walks out in his red suit to a church that's completely silent. TV cameras watch his every move.

Pastor Bart walks to the pew side of the pulpit and stares intensely, unblinking, at his congregation. Those few brave souls who dare make eye contact cower uncomfortably under his penetrating glare.

Pastor Bart walks across the stage and continues boring holes through any person who locks eyes with him. A pen drops and Pastor Bart quickly looks over at the noise. He walks behind the pulpit, hands on its sides, and begins to speak.

"I'm gonna talk to you today about liars. Liars. *Wolves.* The devils the Bible warned us about, whose mouths spew deception and filth."

Bart pauses to look at an usher near the thermostat. "Turn off the AC," he orders.

The usher looks at him for confirmation.

"Go ahead, turn it off! I'm preaching reality today—*I'm preachin' fire.*"

The usher clicks off the air conditioning.

"If anyone in this congregation is scared to hear what fire sounds like when it's preached, please leave."

Nobody moves. Nobody makes a sound.

Bart looks at the collection of reporters seated in the rear. He calls to them mockingly, "Reporters? *Will you be staying?*"

The entire congregation turns in their seats to sneer at the reporters.

The reporters are terrified—not by Bart but by the hundreds of people now staring at them with contempt. As a group, they avoid eye contact with the congregation and remain seated.

The congregation turns back toward Pastor Bart.

"Brothers and sisters, I'm sure you've heard these filthy accusations made against me over the past few days. And if you haven't, let me be the first to tell you."

Silence in the church.

"A lady that I've never met, who I've never even *seen*, and who I wouldn't know from Adam and Eve decided that she was going to take money from this church. From this congregation. From my people."

Bart shouts, *"From God's people!"*

Bart's voice echoes throughout the church.

"And the truth is, I wouldn't know her from Adam and Eve because she's neither. This woman is a *snake*. A *liar.*"

"POISON!" Bart yells as he stomps his foot.

In the stillness of the church, reporters are heard quickly scribbling down notes.

"What are you writing back there?" Bart asks sarcastically.

A few young reporters look up from their notepads.

Bart challenges them, "Huh? What are you guys writing?"

The congregation turns back and stares again. The reporters stop writing as they face off with hundreds of people eyeing them suspiciously.

Bart continues in a challenging tone, "Are you writin' lies? Lies about me and *lies about this church?*"

One young reporter panics and breaks ranks as he shakes his head in response to Bart.

Bart pounces on him, "You! What are you writing?!"

The young reporter is completely out of his league. "The truth," he says meekly.

Bart's eyes flash, "Ahh, *the truth!* That's right young man, you *are* writing the truth today because I'm tellin' it."

The church is getting hot now. A few people in the middle pews fan themselves.

Pastor Bart suddenly leaves the stage and heads down the aisle toward the front doors of the church, a mobile camera chasing close behind. Bart exits through the doors as the breathless congregation watches on the church's big screen monitors.

Light rain falls outside as two teenagers flirt with one another in front of the church. Pastor Bart suddenly arrives in their presence and glares at them as they stand frozen in fright. A gust of wind blows rain onto Pastor Bart as he stares them down.

Pastor Bart re-enters the church and stomps down the aisle toward the stage. As the mobile camera follows him, he yells a command to his doormen.

"Doormen! Close the doors! Lock 'em and bar 'em!"

Big John and Rich quickly move to close and lock the doors as Pastor Bart stomps determinedly back to the pulpit. Bart's building a sweat as he stares out over his congregation.

"Brothers and sisters, *these doors* are closed to liars. *These doors* are closed to sowers of sin."

Bart's voice builds, *"These doors* do not admit adulterers and they don't admit *whores!"*

Bart pauses.

"You, girl! Whatever your name is!"

Another pause.

"Your ticket into this church is *null and void*. We don't want you!"

He stomps out the words, "I-don't-want-you!"

Pastor Bart shouts as he pounds the pulpit, "GOD-DOESN'T-WANT-YOU!"

A brave female voice from the congregation shouts, "Amen!"

Bart hears the voice and steps back from the pulpit to take a breath. He's sweating profusely.

"Amen!" shouts another lady. A cascade of female *Amens* follow.

The congregation returns to silence as the reporters scribble. It's now very hot inside the church. Many people are sweating and fanning themselves.

Bart paces back and forth behind the pulpit. He wipes sweat from his brow and returns to the pulpit to speak.

"Reporters!" he yells. "You asked for my comment. Here it is."

The reporters stop writing and look up at Bart.

"That filthy, lying whore will receive *no* money from my congregation, my church, or me."

The congregation starts to buzz and *Amens* are heard.

"And if she's wise, she'll repent for her sins. She'll go running to Jesus just as fast as she can!"

Light applause breaks out in the pews.

"Because if she doesn't, that poor girl is in for a serious wake-up call—God doesn't like *liars!*"

The congregation takes to their feet with enthusiastic applause for their Pastor.

"And if that lost little girl keeps up her wickedness, keeps spreadin' her lies," Bart raises a finger to emphasize, "God might just decide one day to *strike her down with a bolt of lightning!*"

The pulpit microphone suddenly hisses and snaps over the PA system. Bart angrily grabs the mic and instantly becomes stuck to it. He begins to shake and wail horrendously as the congregation roars with applause. From the band area, Joey shoots to his feet with morbid fascination painting his face.

On live television, Pastor Bart Baxter is being electrocuted by a microphone while his unwitting congregation applauds and cheers him on.

Through Bart's eyes, the pews are filled with devils who delight at his electrocution. They giggle and prance as his veins sizzle. Only one human is seen—Luke in the front row, head bowed and sobbing.

A loud bang is heard as the circuit breaker blows and Bart is thrown backward onto the stage. His lifeless body lies smoking as the bottoms of his shoes face the congregation. One shoe still has gum stuck to the bottom.

Epilogue

A song:
　　Come to Jesus, He's waiting for you
　　Come to Jesus, He's asking you to
　　Come to Jesus, He'll dry all your tears
　　Come to Jesus, He'll fix all your fears
　　You know that old dirty Devil is tryin' and tryin'
　　He's selling us lies for our souls, I ain't buyin'
　　Pick a side, but know the cost (know the cost)
　　Cause if you choose wrong, your soul is lost (oh it's lost)
　　Come to Jesus, the Savior of Man
　　Come to Jesus, everyone can
　　Come to Jesus, He'll make you whole
　　Come to Jesus, He'll save your soul
　　You know that old dirty Devil is tryin' and tryin'
　　He's selling us lies for our souls, I ain't buyin'
　　Pick a side, but know the cost (know the cost)
　　Cause if you choose wrong, your soul is lost (oh it's lost)
　　Don't choose wrong (no don't choose wrong)
　　Don't choose wrong (don't do it, don't do it)
　　Don't choose wrong (oh please, don't choose wrong)
　　Don't choose wrong (don't do it, don't do it)

Ron Johnson is the creator of the satirical blog *The Jim Bakker Food-bucket Fanpage*. He is a native of Long Beach, California, where he was raised by wolves from an early age. Ron currently resides in Boulder, Colorado, with his wife and two dogs.

Ron's hobbies include listening to and playing music, organic gardening, and cracking imaginary eggs on the heads of his wife and dogs.

www.ingramcontent.com/pod-product-compliance
Lightning Source LLC
Chambersburg PA
CBHW050451110726
47899CB00003B/896